E. Lorraine, Charles P. Stone

The Central Water-Line from the Ohio River to the Virginia Capes

connecting the Kanawha and James Rivers, affording the shortest outlet of

navigation from the Mississippi basin to the Atlantic

E. Lorraine, Charles P. Stone

The Central Water-Line from the Ohio River to the Virginia Capes
connecting the Kanawha and James Rivers, affording the shortest outlet of
navigation from the Mississippi basin to the Atlantic

ISBN/EAN: 9783337409784

Printed in Europe, USA, Canada, Australia, Japan

Cover: Foto ©Andreas Hilbeck / pixelio.de

More available books at **www.hansebooks.com**

THE

CENTRAL WATER-LINE

FROM THE

OHIO RIVER

TO THE

VIRGINIA CAPES,

CONNECTING THE

KANAWHA AND JAMES RIVERS,

AFFORDING THE SHORTEST OUTLET OF NAVI-
GATION FROM THE MISSISSIPPI BASIN
TO THE ATLANTIC.

———•◦•———

RICHMOND, VA.
PRINTED BY GARY & CLEMMITT.
1868.

NECESSITY OF A CENTRAL LINE OF NAVIGATION DIRECTLY EASTWARD FROM THE OHIO RIVER TO THE CHESAPEAKE BAY.

Cheap transportation is the great necessity of the west. Its products exceed in amount the means at command of cheap outlet to the seaboard. They press constantly upon the avenues of transportation, and millions of western producers are thus placed under the power of carriers. A system of transportation is needed which shall be free from interruption, and sufficient to carry all the freights promptly and at low charges. The railroads do not furnish this system. Their charges are high, and are put up when the business is most pressing. They are not common highways, but close corporations. Though their rates may be borne for short distances, yet but few of the agricultural and mineral products of the west can bear even their minimum charges over the long distances which intervene between very extensive portions of the far interior and the seaboard. Beyond certain distances from the eastern markets, the great bulk of agricultural and mineral products must rely exclusively upon water transportation.

There are now but two routes of continuous navigation by which they can obtain outlet—that by the northern lakes and that by the Mexican gulf. But these, besides being liable to the casualties of climate (one of them to five months of interruption by ice), are so circuitous, that they require the products of our very extended country to pass beyond its boundaries in seeking their way to its own markets. This tedious circuit, while it is at all times objectionable on the score of time and cost, is most especially so whenever the nation becomes, or is in danger of becoming, involved in hostilities with a maritime power. During the recent war with a domestic power, whose ports were rigidly blockaded, this evil was most sensibly felt, even with reference to the route by the lakes. What might not the evil be in the event of a war with Great Britian?

The great length of these two circuitous lines of water transit, and the non-existence, up to the present time, of any continuous line of navigation directly across the country from the centres of the interior to the centre of the seaboard, have compelled a resort to the policy of substituting railroad transportation over the direct routes. But although the cost of carriage has been much cheapened on these works, they cannot be thrown open to general use and free competition. Meantime water transportation has itself undergone very great improvements, which have had the effect of reducing freights far below any possible minimum at which railroads can afford them. It is now practicable, on lines of unbroken navigation, for the heaviest classes of agricultural and mineral products to be borne, from distances exceeding five thousand miles in the interior, to the seaboard, at charges by no means prohibitory.

Even at present the great bulk of western trade avoids the direct transit across the country afforded by the railroads, and seeks the circuitous and more or less hazardous routes of the lakes and of the gulf, on account of cheapness; thus proving, that as water will seek its *lowest* outlet, however great the circuit it may have to pursue, so trade will seek its *cheapest* outlet, however long may be the passage. It is true, that during the recent war, vast quantities of produce went to market over the railroads; but then, the gulf route was closed and the lake route much obstructed. There was also a stronger reason even than this, which found its cause in the high prices resulting from the condition of the currency and the existence of war. The direction which these phenomena gave to the movement of products is thus accounted for by the superintendent of the census in his report under the department of agriculture:

Had it not been for the high premium on gold, the price of wheat in this country, and especially at the west, would have been less than the cost of production ; as it is, the advance in gold has served to increase prices in the west much more in proportion than in the eastern and middle states. For instance, if a bushel of American wheat sells at $1 25 in London, and the cost of sending it from Iowa is $1, the Iowa farmer, with gold at par, receives only twenty-five cents a bushel for the wheat. Should gold continue at $2 50 (the price at the present writing, 1864), though the wheat still brings only $1 25 per bushel in London, and the cost of sending it there should be $1 per bushel, as before, the Iowa farmer would receive $2 12 per bushel for his wheat instead of twenty-five cents, as would be the case if gold was at par. The wheat is sold for gold, and $1 25 in gold sells for $3 12 in legal money. Deduct $1 as the expense of sending it to London, and we have $2 12 as the price which wheat should bring in Iowa.

In other words, the premium on gold increases the price of wheat in Iowa eight-fold.

This statement of the superintendent of the census, though not accurate in its details, even as of the date when it was written, yet serves to suggest the manner in which war prices, in conjunction with a depreciated currency, may operate temporarily to enable the owners of western produce to pay the high expenses of railroad transportation. With the fall of prices to normal rates, and with the gradual decline of the premium on gold, western producers find themselves obliged to desist from the use of railroads for heavy products for long distances, and again to recur to the circuitous navigation of the lakes and of the gulf. *No interior water-line of continuous east and west navigation yet exists within the United States.*

But if a line of cheap water transportation were opened directly eastward from the centres of western production to the centre of the Atlantic seaboard line, it would offer all the advantages of directness, shortness, expedition, and freedom from interruption, which are presented by the central lines of railroad; combined with the indispensable desideratum of cheapness, now only presented by the circuitous routes of gulf and lake navigation. Such a line would be afforded by completing the unfinished portion of the Virginia canal, over the 80 miles of distance between the present terminus at Buchanan, Botetourt county, Virginia, and the Greenbrier river, in Greenbrier county, West Virginia. This work would connect steamboat navigation at Richmond with steamboat navigation on the Kanawha, by a canal 277 miles long; whereas the Erie canal in New York connects steamboat navigation at either end of it by a canal navigation of 363 miles in length.

American genius and enterprise have accomplished many grand achievements for the west; first, the application of steamboat navigation to the Mississippi river and its great tributaries; then the opening of the Erie canal; then the construction of great lines of railroad over the most difficult passes of the Alleghanies at immense cost. One great achievement remains to be performed. It is the opening of a line of water transportation directly eastward across the shortest passage of the Alleghanies, from the Ohio to the base of the Chesapeake. Railroad transportation is for manufacturers, merchants, speculators and capitalists; water transportation is for the people. A line of navigation, open to general use, accessible to all classes, is needed on the shortest route from the interior to the seaboard. That route is presented by the inter-lapping valleys of the Kanawha and James rivers in Virginia, connecting the channel of the Ohio and the channel of the James.

Impressed with the great superiority in cheapness, general utility, and popular convenience, of water navigation over railroad transportation, for their increasing products; and naturally desiring a shorter, more central, and more expeditious line of water transit than the present circuitous and extraneous ones by way of the northern lakes and southern gulf, the people of the west are beginning to look to Congress for the provision of such a route. With this object in view, the General Assembly of Iowa, at its last session, unanimously voted an able and earnest memorial on the subject to the national legislature, following it by a resolution "instructing their senators and requiring their representatives in congress to use their best efforts to obtain such aid from the general government as will secure the early completion" of the Virginia water line.

The memorial concludes as follows:

This is a work of great national importance. Its benefits will be shared directly by more than half the people of this country; and indirectly by all. It is a necessary addition to the improvement of the navigation of the Western rivers, without which the benefits of that measure will be but half realized. It is a work to be done by the whole country for the benefit of the whole country. It belongs to the Government of the United States.

Nothing need to be given. An advance upon good security, for the return of principal and interest is all that will be necessary. Not only will this advance be returned in kind with the interest, but the benefits of each year will return the outlay more than five fold. Instead of increasing our national burthen of taxation it will so increase the means of payment as to greatly lessen it.

To the end then of obtaining government aid, there should be a co-operative movement of cities, towns and States. It should be connected with the western river improvements as a part of the same enterprise, and the influence of the great interest to be promoted by it, should be concentrated through a convention, and brought to bear upon Congress, to ensure a speedy completion. Keeping it always in mind that every year's delay *is a loss of more than five times the amount required for that object.*

Resolved, By the General Assembly of the State of Iowa, That the great rivers on our Eastern and Western borders are the natural highways for the trade and commerce of our State, and any measures that will add to their efficiency and importance, as channels of communication will increase the value of all our productions; add to the price of all real property, and contribute to the prosperity of all our people.

2. That the line of water communication between the Valley of the Mississippi and the Atlantic ocean, by way of the Kanawha and James rivers, through the states of Virginia and West Virginia, is a work of national importance, and one deeply affecting the interest of the grain producing states of the Northwest.

3. That our Senators in Congress be instructed, and our Representatives requested to use their best efforts to obtain such aid from the General Government, as will secure the early completion of said line of water communication.

4. That a copy of these joint resolutions and the accompanying memorial, be forwarded by the Secretary of the State to the President of the United States, the President of the Senate, and to each of our Senators and Representatives in Congress.

RESULTS EFFECTED BY THE ERIE CANAL. OTHERS EQUALLY GREAT WOULD ATTEND THE OPENING OF THE VIRGINIA CANAL.

Although steamboat navigation on the western waters dates from 1817, the development of the west did not fairly begin until 1825. In October of that year the great Erie canal was completed. The effect was virtually to give another mouth to the Mississippi river. It opened to market a vast region which otherwise could have presented but limited attractions to emigration. The fact, that the Lake country, where the rigors of winter are more severe, and the climatic disadvantages imposed upon agriculture greater, than in any part of the Union, has undergone a more rapid development than any other, is due in chief part to the Erie canal. This work brought that great region within readier and cheaper reach of market than any other portion of the west. The long and tortuous channel of the Mississippi, the circuitous navigation of the gulf, and the *heating, sweating* and *moulding* effect of the semi-tropical and moist southern climate upon many products of agriculture, presented objections to the gulf transit, which rendered the lake route preferable to it, even for the trade of localities where the advantage of distance was less considerable. The falls of the Niagara, and rapids of the St. Lawrence river were turned by the canal, which completed a line of unbroken navigation from the farthest of the great lakes to tide-water at Albany. On the completion of the Erie, several canals in the north-west were immediately projected and were soon completed, connecting the lakes with the Ohio river on the south, and the Mississippi river on the west. These, in later years, were followed by railroads laid down in the same directions, forming portages between the navigation of the great rivers and that of the lakes. But all these canals and railroads pointed to the Eric canal as the common *debouche*. These works were all in the first instance constructed as feeders to the Eric canal, which was the parent work and grand trunk line of the whole system. After the system of works, of which the Erie canal was the base, had stimulated an unprecedented development of population and production in the west, it was found incapable of discharging the vast trade which it had created; and then it became necessary to enlarge its capacity, and to construct as many auxiliary works as possible, parallel with it. Hence the Welland and St. Lawrence canals, and hence the Grand Trunk railroad in Canada, and the New York Central, the New York Erie, the Pennsylvania Central, and the Baltimore and Ohio railroads, within the United States. But it may be said with perfect truth, that if there had been no Eric canal, the stupendous agricultural development which has been witnessed in the west would not have taken place, and that these great auxiliary works would not have become necessary until after a much greater lapse of time.

The following table shews the effect of the canal upon the growth of imports, exports and population in the city of New York, in contrast with the same growth in Philadelphia where the influence of the trade of the canal was only partial and indirect:

Year.	Tolls. Amount collected.	TONS. Total movement East and West.	Value of imports at the ports of		Value of exports from the ports of		Population of	
			New York.	Philadelphia.	New York.	Philadelphia.	New York.	Philadelphia.
1820	$5,244	....	....	....	$11,769,511	$5,743,549	123,706	137,097
1830	1,056,922	....	38,556,064	9,525,893	17,666,624	4,291,793	203,007	188,961
1840	1,775,717	1,417,046	60,064,942	8,464,882	32,408,689	6,820,145	312,712	258,832
1850	3,273,899	3,076,617	116,667,558	12,065,834	47,580,357	4,501,606	515,394	409,353

The power of a direct canal running west and east to attract trade to itself is exhibited in the operations of the Eric canal. "There are now seven great railway lines competing with this work, besides the canals of the St. Lawrence. They are the Baltimore and Ohio, the Pennsylvania Central, the Atlantic and Great Western, the Philadelphia and Erie, the Erie, and the New York Central railroads, in the United States, and the Grand Trunk railroad in Canada. Yet these great railways do not (computing with theirs all the trade which goes to Montreal, Ogdensburg and Cape Vincent by lake), secure more than fifty per cent. of the total eastward movement of all classes of freight from the west to the seaboard markets." [Annual statement of trade and commerce of Buffalo for 1865.]

It is a peculiarity of railroads that they stimulate a greater production in the country within their reach than they can transport. Their capacity for transportation falls behind the demands upon it, resulting from the stimulus which they impart to production. This is particularly the case where the roads are of great length, and penetrate into fertile regions of country. The construction of railroads does not relieve the pressure of produce upon the means of transit, but on the contrary, aggravates the pressure.

The opening of another and shorter canal eastward to the seaboard, over a line exempt from the long suspensions enforced further north by winter ice, would produce a similar development of trade on the more southern line; and some future statistician will be able to write of the Virginia canal, as the superintendent of the census has written of the Erie:

"The opening of this work was the announcement of a new era in the internal grain trade of the United States. To the pioneer, the agriculturist and the merchant, the grand avenue developed a new world. From that period do we date the rise and progress of the northwest, as well as the development of the internal grain trade."

INADEQUACY OF ALL EXISTING OUTLETS FOR TRANSPORTING THE INCREASING TRADE OF THE WEST.

Remarking upon the subject of transportation for western trade, the superintendent of the census says:

"It is feared by many in New York that the construction of a ship canal to the St. Lawrence river would damage the canal interests of the state by diverting a large portion of the grain trade of the lakes from the Erie canal; but when it is considered that the production of grain in the northwestern states increased from 218,463,583 bushels in 1840 to 642,120,366 bushels in 1860; and that of the eight food-producing states west of the lakes, embracing an area of 262,549,000 acres, only about 52,000,000 acres were under cultivation in 1860, and that 26,000,000 acres of that have been broken since 1850, no fears need be entertained that any of the outlets to the ocean will be unoccupied to the extent of their capacity. *The only fear is, that we will not keep pace with the increased production by the provision of increased facilities of transportation.*"

Sir Morton Peto, in his interesting and very clever work on the Resources and Prospects of America, makes the following truthful observations:

"How far is the amount of tonnage employed in inland intercourse in America adequate to the wants of the country? In considering this point we have to regard the very great lengths over which traffic has to be carried; and looking at those distances, no reasonable doubt can be entertained that *the inland navigation of America is very inadequate to the wants of the people. It has not, in fact, kept pace with the population and progress of the country;* and if it were not for the railroads, the great producing districts of the United States would be at a stand still for want of means of transport for their produce. There is a period of the year when the canals are frozen up. The whole task of conveyance then falls upon the railways; and the consequence is, not only an immediate rise in their rates, but absolute inability to conduct the traffic. The results are often most disastrous. In one case 40,000 barrels of flour were detained at Toledo (nearly half way between Chicago and New York) for several months, in consequence of want of carriage. A vast mass of produce is yearly destroyed from the inability of the carriers to forward it. The owners are ruined, and parties in the eastern states, who advance money on this produce, charge excessive rates to cover the risks of delay. *The grain producers of the western states are quite unable to find sufficient means of conveyance for their products,* because the railroads from west to east are choked with traffic. The existing railroad requirements of the west are, in fact, insufficient. At present, because they cannot carry the produce, the whole traffic of the country is subject to two gigantic evils, arising, first, from uncertainty of conveyance; and second, from uncertainty of charge. The present railways are quite insufficient for the growing traffic. The lines of communication from the west by canal, &c., which existed previously to railways, *have not been affected by their construction. The produce of the western states has, in fact, increased faster than the means of transport, and additional facilities for the conveyance of goods are urgently required.* It is of the utmost importance to the development of the west *that no time should be lost in making this additional provision.* An inadequate railroad provision and a corresponding uncertainty as to conveyance and delivery of freights, must have the effect of checking production in the west, and consequently, of checking capital of the east from seeking employment in the west. Railway facilities are now the measure of the prosperity of the country.

"Now, what is the effect of this inadequacy of transportation? The producer, the merchant, the railway company and the consumer, are all directly injured; but the indirect injury extends far beyond those interests. The whole produce of the west, and consequently the entire cultivation of America, is affected. If the produce cannot be carried, it can only find local markets. If it only finds local markets, prices must abate. If prices abate, the stimulus to the cultivation of land is lost. If the land is not required for cultivation, in the same proportion it necessarily diminishes in value. The prosperity of the west, the value of its produce, the value of its land, and the extent of land cultivated—*all depend, therefore, upon increased facilities for the conveyance of produce*, and those facilities canals and railroads must afford. The American public ought never to be satisfied until they are able to calculate on fixed moderate prices for freight, and fixed periods for its delivery. The future of the west depends upon ample means of communication with the east; and the success of its means of communication with the east is expressed in a few words, 'Prompt and economical delivery—in a fixed time and at a fixed price.'"

Nothing could be more true than these remarks. The talk of competition between railroads and canals, between one water line and another, or one railroad line and another, is wholly out of place. When there is more than enough trade for all, it is useless to consider the subject of competing interests.

A direct unbroken line of water transportation is urgently needed for the teeming products of the west. The necessity for it is becoming more and more imperious every year. How vast is the country producing tonnage, how wonderfully prolific is its production, how marvelously rapid its increase!!

Vast extent of Country to be Drained.

The portion of the Mississippi valley and Lake country interested in the opening of a direct line of transportation extending the navigation of the Ohio and Mississippi to the base of Chesapeake bay, is composed of the following states and territories, whose area and population, taken chiefly from the census of 1860, are attached:

	Sq. Miles.		Population.
West Virginia,	24,000		376,688
Kentucky,	37,080		1,155,684
Tennessee,	45,000		826,782
Arkansas,	52,198		435,450
Ohio,	39,964		2,339,511
Indiana,	33,809		1,350,428
Illinois,	55,409		1,711,951
Michigan,	56,213		709,113
Wisconsin,	53,924		775,881
Minnesota,	83,531		172,023
Iowa,	55,000		674,913
Missouri,	65,039		1,182,012
Kansas,	83,000		107,206
Nebraska,	70,000		28,841
Dakota,	220,000	(1865)	4,837
Montana,	150,000	(1865)	20,000
Colorada,	104,000		34,277
Total,	1,228,795		11,945,597

In the same geographical relations to trade and its markets, though not belonging to the same political jurisdiction, is another extensive region lying above our natural boundary line. The Red river of the north, and the Sascatchawan, in Northwest British America, traverse a territory in the heart of the continent, five hundred thousand square miles in extent, and capable of sustaining a population of thirty millions. "In the valleys of the Sascatchawan and Assiniboin," Professor Hand estimates that "there are eleven millions of acres of arable land of the first quality." Of this region about one half is prairie and one half is wood land; it is the only extensive prairie country open to the Canadas east of the Rocky mountains; it is destined to be the Illinois or Iowa of British America. This is no inhospitable desert repugnant to the increase of the human race. Here is "a vast wedge-shaped tract of country, extending from 47 degrees to 60 degrees of northern latitude, 10 degrees of longitude, deep at the base, containing 500,000 square miles of habitable land subject to few and inconsiderable variations in climate. The summer at Buffalo is about ninety-five days, and it is ninety days at Cumberland House on the Sascatchawan, on 54 degrees north. The annual mean temperature is only 8 degrees lower than Toronto, with 17 inches more of rain and 33 inches less of snow, than at Toronto. Herds of buffalo winter on the wood-land as far north as 60 degrees parallel. Corn grows on both sides of the Sascatchawan; wheat sown in the Red river valley in May is gathered in by the end of August.

The lake and river system of this region are almost as wonderful as our own; lake Winnepeg having an area equal to that of lake Ontario, and lake Manitohah nearly half that of Winnepeg. The distance from a given point on the westerly end of lake Superior to the navigable waters of Frazier's river in British Columbia, will not exceed 2,000 miles, about twice the distance between Boston and Chicago. The westerly end of lake Superior is on the parallel of about 46 degrees, which passes from the heart of Germany through the British channel, across the gulf of St. Lawrence, lake Superior, Vancouver's island, and the rich and populous archipelago of Japan.

The climate of Edmonton is milder in winter than at St. Paul. The Sascatchawan is clear of ice in the spring as soon as the Mississippi is, between St. Anthony and Galena. Steamboat navigation, now established on the Red river of the north to Fort Gerry, by Americans, can readily be extended through lake Winnepeg and up the Sascatchawan, to Fort Edmonton, the supposed eastern limit to the new gold district. This territory has now a population of about ten thousand. The valley of the Red river of the north will make one of the finest of wheat growing countries, the yield being forty to sixty bushels to the acre. One hundred miles east of the Rocky mountains, on the Sascatchawan, is an immense coal field, stretching away towards the Arctic ocean.

The trade of all this region, equal in area to ten states of the size of New York, will, from necessity, seek an outlet by the Mississippi, or lake Superior, or the Virginia water-line. The discovery of gold will ensure its early settlement.

Its probable Population.

Here is a great region within and bordering upon the United States, embracing 1,750,000 squares miles of territory, becoming rapidly populated, whose trade is to be brought to the seaboard. The population of the portion of it which lies within the United States has greatly increased since the census of 1860, and will continue to increase until this expanded region, one of the most fertile in the world, shall contain inhabitants approximating in numbers, per square mile, the populations of other districts of the earth no more fertile. As indicating the actual density of population in other quarters of the globe, the following table is given:

Number of Inhabitants to the Square Mile.

Belgium	397,		Prussia	159,
Saxony	353,		Bavaria	156,
Eng. and Wales	307,		Austria	142,
Netherlands	250,		Hanover	123,
Sardinia	225,		Denmark	114,
Wurtemburg	210,		Scotland	92,
Ireland	205,		Sweden	21,
German states	199,		Norway	13,
France	176,			

Few, if any, of these European states are more fertile than the valleys of the Mississippi and the lakes; many of them are far less fertile. It is, therefore, quite reasonable to assume that within another century the population of this region will average one hundred persons to the square mile, and will reach the imposing aggregate of one hundred and seventy-five millions of inhabitants.

The state of Illinois gained, between 1850 and 1860, one hundred per cent. of population. To show how much room is open for an increase of population, one of the densest portions of the population of the west, that embracing the states of Indiana, Illinois, Michigan, Wisconsin, Iowa and Minnesota numbered, in 1860, only sixteen persons to the square mile. The increase of population in the entire Union during each of the last decades was 35½ per cent. At a rate of increase for the west, equal to only 33 per cent. (it will be more than 50), the population of the seventeen states and territories of the west that have been named, will be one hundred and twenty millions by 1940. But the increase will be much more rapid. There are persons now born who will live to see it reach more than that number.

But confining our attention to the affairs of the present time, it is important to know what amount of tonnage is now produced in the states and territories under consideration; what portion of this production is necessary for consumption, and what part might be spared for market; whether all that might be spared does or does not actually go to market, and if it does not go, whether the failure is due or not to inadequate facilities of transport, and too great a cost of carriage.

Its Production in Tons.

In 1860, the production of that portion of the west embraced in the seventeen states and territories entering into the questions under discussion, was as follows:

Wheat, bushels,	111,119,374	equal to	3,367,700 tons.
Corn, bushels,	527,893,527	do.	15,996,775 do.
Rye, bushels,	5,568,461		167,529 do.
Oats, bushels,	71,962,329		1,151,397 do.
Barley, bushels,	5,210,770 ⎫		
Buckwheat, bushels,	4,286,566 ⎭		226,127 do.
Beans and Peas, bushels,	1,648,538 ⎫		
Irish Potatoes, bushels,	39,015,910 ⎬		1,285,810 do.
Sweet Potatoes, bushels,	4,981,759 ⎭		
Clover seed, bushels,	403,423		
Grass seed, bushels,	546,170		
Flax seed, bushels,	337,818		
Butter, pounds,	183,634,188		91,317 do.
Cheese, pounds,	28,575,219		14,287 do.
Wool, pounds,	28,267,123		14,133 do.
Flax, pounds,	2,130,823		1,065 do.
Tobacco, pounds,	222,329,886		111,165 do.
Hops, pounds,	272,892		136 do.
Maple sugar, pounds,	12,164,546		6,082 do.
Honey, pounds,	10,857,944		5,428 do.
Beeswax, pounds,	476,939		236 do.
Hay, tons,			7,405,376
Hemp, tons,			68,902
Coal, tons,			1,928,466
Pig Iron, tons,			163,266
Copper, tons,			7,422
Orchard produce, value,	$7,431,517		
Market garden produce, value,	3,695,696		
Home manufactures, value,	9,774,577		
Slaughtered animals, value,	99,837.933	equal to	713,128 tons.
Lead, value,	915,481	do.	4,577 do.
Salt, value,	3,620,418	do.	250.000 do.
Fisheries, value,	351,479	do.	5,859 do.
Lumber, value,	35,429,729	do.	5,250 do.
Wine, gallons,	975,254		
Maple molasses, gallons,	1,108,772		
Sorghum molasses, gallons,	5,620,675		
Grand total,			32,991,433 tons.

Here is a grand aggregate of thirty-three millions of tonnage. It is difficult to determine what amount of this total could be

spared from consumption and sent to market. Some statisticians
contend that a community occupying so fertile a country, and so
situated, as that of the great west, can easily spare for market
an amount of tonnage equal to three-fifths of the total production;
which, in the case of the west, and its production in 1860, would be
twenty millions of tons. This estimate does not seem excessive
when we find from the foregoing statement, that if we deduct for
home consumption a tonnage equivalent to that of all the oats, all
the hay (besides every other sort of fodder), all the butter and
cheese, and orchard and garden produce, all home manufactures,
all the wine, molasses, fish, clover and grass seeds, hops, maple sugar, honey and beeswax, all the wool, flax and hemp, all the coal
and pig iron, three-fourths of all slaughtered animals, and of
the irish and sweet potatoes, peas and beans, five pounds of tobacco
for each inhabitant, and six bushels of wheat to every man, woman
and child of the population, there would still be eighteen millions
of tons left to be sent to market, besides what live stock might go
off, on the hoof, by rail, or by boat. Such was the amount of tonnage which the west would seem to have been competent to send
to the seaboard in 1860, if the facilities at hand for carrying it to
market had been adequate in capacity to the herculean task, and
if the rates of charge had been low enough to leave a profit to the
producer.

Why did not this Tonnage come to Market?

But these facilities were not adequate in capacity, nor were the
charges of transit sufficiently low, to permit so vast an eastward
movement of tonnage. In a comparative sense, the actual movement of tonnage as late as 1862, while the stimulus of war prices
was active in bringing it forward, was very meagre.

"In 1862," says the report of the Board of Trade and Commerce
of Buffalo, 1865, "the surplus products of the west sent eastward
(*through* trade) to the tide water markets, including products of
wood, agriculture, animals, manufactures and miscellaneous commodities, was 5,176,499 tons. This includes the eastward movement of through freight over the four great roads of the United
States, and the Grand Trunk and Northern railways, and the total
exports from Buffalo and Oswego by canal. If the way freights received at the western terminal points of all these railways, and delivered in the interior, be added to the *through* freight, it is esti-

mated that the total number of tons moved out of the west during that year exceeded 5,500,000. Of the eastward movement in 1862, 2,080,656, were sent from Buffalo, and 638,419 tons from Oswego, *making nearly fifty per cent. of the total movement by the New York canals*, and the remaining portion by the five through lines of railroad."

Thus, it seems, that the great public works of the country already in operation, did not attract from their places of production, nor transport, one-third of the products which the west could actually have spared. If the whole exportable production had offered itself for transit, it could not have been carried; and it did not offer itself; because the cost of carriage on a vast proportion of the exportable products was not low enough to tempt them forward.

PROBABLE INCREASE OF THIS TONNAGE.

Now, while the number and capacity of these works have been very slightly augmented, production in the west has grown apace. That this production grows at about an equal rate with the population, is shewn by the following table for the country embracing Ohio, Indiana, Illinois, Missouri, Iowa, Minnesota, Wisconsin and Michigan:

	Population.	Cereal Product.
1840,	3,340,542	165,698,832 bushels.
1850,	5,403,595	310,050,295 bushels.
1860,	8,855,932	556,801,897 bushels.

The decennial increase in these states both of population and cereal production, exceeded sixty-five per cent. The actual exportation of the west in 1862, slightly exceeded five millions of tons. Distinguishing actual from possible exportation, the actual movement from the west, if it shall increase at equal pace with the population, will by 1880, become fifteen millions. How will this certain amount of exportable tonnage find exit? Unless the bulk of it go down the Mississippi, it will be unable to reach the seaboard, without a great increase in the number and capacity of our public works. Even on the basis of actual exportations, a direct canal across the shortest passage of the Alleghanies to the seaboard, is evidently necessary.

But, by 1880, the exportation will be far more than fifteen millions
2

of tons, provided means are provided for carrying away the produce. In 1860, when the population was twelve millions, the west *could* have exported eighteen millions of tons. In the absence of facilities of cheap transportation, it actually did export less than five millions of tons. There was a difference of two hundred and fifty per cent. between the actual and possible exportation. At present the western population has reached eighteen millions, and it is capable of exporting fully twenty-five millions of tons of produce, if avenues of transportation were accessible. and if freights were cheap. To bring out this trade a short line of cheap *navigation* is necessary. Another canal on the most direct central route, with the attendant railroads that would spring up near its margin, is indispensable to the accommodation and development of western trade.

Comparative value and capacity of Canals and Railroads.

Much has been said of the comparitive merits of canals and railroads. When the discussion loses sight of distance and circumstances, it leads to no sound conclusion. The chief exports of the west are the bulky products of the farm, forest and mine, and it is generally true, that beyond certain distances, these commodities cannot afford the cost of railroad transportation. For instance, if a cent and a'half a ton per mile (which is much below the average charge), be assumed as the lowest price at which railroads can profitably transport tonnage; and if the specie price of wheat in market be $1 50 per bushel, or $49 50 per ton of 33 bushels; and if the cost of growing wheat be 60 cents per bushel or $19 80 per ton, so that the margin between cost and market value is 90 cents per bushel, or $29 70 per ton; then, making no allowance for expenses of handling, storage, commissions and the like, it is clear that wheat cannot go farther than 1980 miles by railway without the cost of carriage trenching upon cost of producing.

Price per ton in market,	$49 50
Cost per ton of growing the crop,	19 80
Margin for expenses of carriage,	$29 70

Equal, at 1½ cents per ton per mile to, 1980 miles.

But, as the cost of production varies in different localities, and even on different farms, and as the price in market varies almost weekly, it would not be proper to conclude either that railroads can invariably carry wheat as far as 1980 miles, or that this is the distance beyond which wheat can never be transported, in any season, under any state of the markets, between any points. It is generally true, that in a region so remote from the seaboard as vast portions of the west, water transportation is essential to the purposes of farmers, lumbermen, and miners of bulky minerals; while railroads suit best the uses of manufacturers, merchants and speculators. Both methods of transportation are necessary, each for its appropriate sort of trade, and so far from being antagonistic, they are mutually assistant and beneficial. Cheap navigation developes production in the first instance; and then commerce and art demand the assistance of railroads for their more rapid operations.

The respective distances for which canals, railroads, and ordinarp highways command trade is approximately exhibited by the following table. It takes no account of charges other than for freight; and is made out for wheat at $1 50 per bushel, or $49 50 per ton, and corn at 75 cents per bushel, or $24 75 per ton of 33 bushels. It assumes the cost of carriage at five mills per ton per mile on canals, fifteen mills on railroads, and fifteen cents on ordinary highways:

Statement showing the value of a ton of Wheat and one of Corn at given distances from market, as affected by cost of transportation respectively by canal, by railroad, and over the ordinary highway.

	Canal Carriage.		Railway Carriage.		Common Road Carriage.	
	Wheat.	Corn.	Wheat.	Corn.	Wheat.	Corn.
Value at market..........................	49.50	24.75	49.50	24.75	49.50	24.75
" 10 miles from market.........	49.45	24.70	49.35	24.60	48.00	23.25
" 20 " " "	49.40	24.65	49.20	24.45	46.50	21.75
" 30 " " "	49.35	24.60	49.05	24.30	45.00	20.25
" 40 " " "	49.30	24.55	48.90	24.15	43.50	18.75
" 50 " " "	49.25	24.50	48.75	24.00	42.00	17.25
" 60 " " "	49.20	24.45	48.60	23.85	40.50	15.75
" 70 " " "	49.15	24.40	48.45	23.70	39.00	14.25
" 80 " " "	49.10	24.35	48.30	23.55	37.50	14.75
" 90 " " "	48.05	24.30	48.15	23.40	36.00	11.25
" 100 " " "	48.00	24.25	48.00	23.25	34.50	9.75
" 110 " " "	47.95	24.20	47.85	23.10	33.00	8.25
" 120 " " "	47.90	24.15	47.70	22.95	31.50	6.75
" 130 " " "	47.85	24.10	47.55	22.80	30.00	5.25
" 140 " " "	47.80	24.05	47.40	22.65	28.50	3.75
" 150 " " "	47.75	24.00	47.25	22.50	27.00	2.25
" 160 " " "	47.70	23.95	47.10	22.35	25.50	.75
" 170 " " "	47.65	23.90	46.95	22.20	24.00	
" 320 " " "	46.90	23.20	44.70	19.95	1 50	
" 330 " " "	46.85	23.15	44.55	19.80		
" 340 " " "	46.80	23.10	44.40	19:65		
" 350 " " " ....;.	46.75	23.05	44.25	19.50		
" 1000 " " "	44.50	19.75	34.50	9.75		
" 1650 " " "	41.25	16.50	24.75			
" 1980 " " "	39.60	14.85	19.80			
" 3300 " " "	33.00	8.25				
" 4950 " " "	24.75					
" 5940 " " "	19.80					
" 9900 " " "						

The table is merely theoretical. Of course the charges on produce, other than for carriage proper, would materially curtail the distances indicated by it. The exhibit is valuable, however, as showing by contrast, for how much greater distances navigation commands trade than overland methods of transit. At 330 miles, the cost of carriage on *common roads* consumes the whole value of wheat, leaving nothing at all for the farmer. At 1,980 miles the freight on *railroads* leaves but 60 cents per bushel ($19 80 per ton) for the grower; and at 3,300 miles sweeps off the total value. But on *canals*, the cost of carriage does not trench upon the cost for production (of 60 cents per bushel) until the wheat has been carried 5,940 miles; nor is the value wholly exhausted within a distance of 9,900 miles.

Thus, the question involved in this comparison is very far from being one of mere per centage. The railroad charges become prohibitory within actual practical distances from the seaboard; and it then becomes a question, with the interior producer, between water transportation and no transportation at all. If no cheap navigation is available, the crops of the far interior must rot in the fields, and the minerals must remain indefinitely emboweled in the earth.

It is very far from being the fact, therefore, that, in a country of such vast extent as ours, railroads have superseded, or can supersede, canals. In a small island like Great Britain they may do so; but not on this spacious continent. Here, canals have not ceased, and they cannot cease, to be of essential importance to the great producing classes of the far interior.

GROWTH OF THE WESTERN GRAIN TRADE. ITS EFFECT UPON OUR FOREIGN EXPORTS OF BREAD STUFFS. NATURAL PREFERENCE OF THIS TRADE AMONG LINES OF OUTLET TO THE SEABOARD.

Forty years ago the surplus products of Ohio had accumulated beyond the means of transport, and wheat sold in the interior at 37 cents per bushel, and Indian corn at 10 cents. Then the Erie canal was opened, and soon after the Ohio canals, and prices were raised more than 50 per cent. Now that the means of transport have been increased, the price of flour at Cincinnati is nearly double the price in 1826, the price of Indian corn is four times, and the price of pork three times as great. On the other hand, the prices of grain and meat on the seaboard have not been reduced in the least. It is therefore evident that the bulk of the gain obtained by the increased facility of transport has gone to the producer.

Not only has the transport of produce been cheapened, but also the cost of the transport of every article of manufacture required by the producer. Machinery and articles of foreign growth have been supplied him at almost seaboard prices. Sugar and coffee were no dearer at Cincinnati in 1860 than in 1835, although the population of the western states in that interval had increased in enormous proportions.

Prior to the opening of the Erie canal the only outlet to the ocean from the northwestern territory was by the river Mississippi. During the progress of the Erie canal it was predicted that "it would never pay," for that the trade would follow the rivers, and was not likely to be diverted across the continent. It has turned out, however, that the artificial channels of trade, the canals and railroads, have completely diverted the course of the traffic as to a very large section of the west. There are various causes for this. The principal, no doubt, is the increase of the grain consuming population in the states of the Atlantic. Other causes are to be found in the uncertainty of river navigation during the summer months, the greater speed and security of transport by railway, the superior advantages of New York to New Orleans as a place of trade; and the greater risk of damage to grain and flour by "heating" in the southern latitudes of the gulf of Mexico. Thus it results that New Orleans has not become a leading shipping port for grain, although her trade in cotton, sugar and tobacco has largely increased.

Much has also been due to the energy of the north; and the graphically expressed complaint of Prof. De Bow was well grounded when he declared, that "the bold, vigorous and sustained effort of the north has succeeded in reversing the very law of nature's God, rolled back the tide of the Mississippi and its ten thousand tributary streams, until their mouths, practically and commercially, are more at New York than at New Orleans."

The first shipments of grain on the lakes, of which there is any record, was made in the year 1836, when the brig John H. McKenzie shipped at Grand Haven, Michigan, 3,000 bushels of wheat for the port of Buffalo.

The first shipment of grain from Chicago, consisting of 78 bushels of wheat in 39 sacks, was made in 1838. The first shipments from the state of Wisconsin were made three years later, in 1841. These shipments consisted of about 4,000 bushels of wheat purchased at Milwaukie on Canadian account.

In 1848 the Illinois and Michigan canal was completed, opening up another great field of cultivation in the state of Illinois. In 1849 the era of railroad communication was inaugurated by the opening of the Chicago and Galena Union railroad, traversing a widely cultivated district. This line of railroad led to a great and rapid development of the country which it traversed. In 1863 nearly *eleven and a half million* bushels of grain were carried over this line. These large shipments of grain to the seaboard soon began to excite an export movement.

The growth of the grain trade of the lakes is illustrated by the following table of

Shipments Eastward from Michigan Ports.

Year.	Bushels.
1858	27,879,293
1859	25,829,753
1860	43,211,448
1861	69,489,113
1862	78,214.675
1863	74,710,664

Such a record of progress is probably unparalleled. The production of grain in the northwestern states is estimated to have increased from 218,463,583 bushels in 1840 to 642,120,366 bushels in 1860.

Thus the opening of the Erie canal in 1825, which placed the Hudson river in communication with lake Erie, inaugurated a new era in the trade of the United States. The shores of the great lakes were brought by this line of communication into connexion with the Atlantic by a navigable water-course through the entire state of New York. This grand avenue did, indeed, "develope a new world to the pioneer, the agriculturist and the merchant."

The following official table shews the ratio of increase in the value of the grain exported from the United States, for a period of 40 years:

Years.	Aggregate value of exports of grain.	Per centage of increase.
1823 to 1833	$67,842,211	
1833 to 1843	73,303,440	8.0
1843 to 1853	198,594,871	170.9
1853 to 1863	512,380,514	158.0

EUROPE BEGINS TO RELY CHIEFLY ON AMERICA FOR GRAIN.

The repeal of the corn laws of Great Britain in 1846 gave the greatest encouragement to the exportation of American grain. During the years 1862 and 1863 the total exports of grain, flour and meal from the United States were of greater value, in either year, than the aggregate value of the whole grain trade of the Union for the ten years from 1833 to 1843.

Year.	Bushels.	Value.
1862	76,309,425	$83,692,812
1863	77,396,082	88,597,064

The years, during which this very great supply of food was exported, were, it should be remembered, years of civil war. Of the total amount of the exports, nearly two-thirds were shipped to Great Britain and Ireland. The proportion sent there is represented as follows:

Year.	Bushels.	Value.
1862,	34,102,735,	$47,916 266
1863,	47,082,026,	56,059 360

The supply of wheat from the United States to England and Ireland during the years 1861, 62, and 63, was estimated to amount to 37½ per cent. of their whole import. Of the imports of flour into Great Britain, 58.3 per cent. were from the United States.

It has been estimated by the *Mark Lane Express*, a paper of authority on agricultural matters, that the average consumption of wheat in Great Britain is six bushels per head per annum; and as the population amounts in round numbers to thirty millions, this gives a total annual consumption of 180,000,000 bushels, and indicates the importance of Great Britain as a customer of our western states. The exportations of wheat from eastern Europe to its western populations having reached their maximum magnitude, and being henceforth destined to decline, while the western European populations are steadily increasing; the dependence of the latter upon American grain is becoming more and more absolute, and the Mississippi valley is becoming more and more emphatically, "the granary of Europe." The rapid growth of our foreign exportations of grain will require, more and more imperatively, the opening of a direct water-line of navigation, from the central west to the seaboard, over the shortest possible line.

Western exportations are even at present much restricted on account of insufficient facilities of cheap transportation ; and this restriction directly affects the foreign produce exportations of the Union. Since the great loss which the export trade of the United States has sustained from the decline of southern production, it has become doubly important to the national prosperity that its exports of western produce should be increased by every possible means. The nation must look chiefly to the free labor of the west for compensation for the sacrifices it has incurred by emancipation. That is the only source from which compensation can come in the form of exportations. These can be indefinitely enhanced by multiplying the channels of cheap transportation from the interior to the seaboard; and, of all such channels which can be possibly devised, none offers so many advantages as the Virginia water-line.

CHEAP TRANSPORTATION MAKES WESTERN TRADE PREFER THE WATER OUTLETS.

Notwithstanding the strong tendency of western produce to seek markets by direct eastward routes, it is still diverted to the circuitous northern or southern water lines by the cheapness of water transportation, and dearness of railroad carriage. This strong tendency of trade to pursue the shortest route eastward to market, has for forty years given the lake and Erie route a great advantage over that by way of New Orleans. These two routes are subject to equivalent disadvantages; that by way of New Orleans to the damaging effect of excessive heat during the summer months upon produce; and that by way of the lakes to obstruction by ice in the winter. These disadvantages being nearly equivalent, the northern route secures more trade by reason of its being much shorter. If the direct railroads were liable to five months of obstruction in their operations, they would fail to secure any considerable proportion of *through* trade, and would be unable to carry *through* produce at prices which it could afford to pay.

WESTERN TRADE PREFERS THE SHORTER NORTHERN WATER OUTLET TO THE LONGER SOUTHERN ONE.

The advantage which its comparative shortness gives to the lake route, over that of the gulf, is exhibited by the statistics of the eastward movement of produce from the west; some of which are now given.

Andrews' Report on "*Colonial and Lake Trade*," gives the eastward movement of tonnage in 1851 as follows:

	Tons.	Value.
By New York canals	1,977,151	$53,727,508
By " " railroads	228,107	11,405,350
By St. Lawrence river	329,631	9,153,589
By Mississippi river	1,292,670	108,051,708

It seems that more tons went by the canals; but more *value* by the Mississippi; owing to the difference in price between farm produce and cotton.

The same authority gives a table of the *value* of property received at the seaboard by way of the Hudson and by way of the Mississippi, for the ten years ending with 1851. The totals for the ten years were as follows:

By way of the Hudson	$484,924,474
By " " Mississippi	857,658,164

Here, too, although the *value* of the movement by the Mississippi was 85 per cent. greater, the avoirdupois *tonnage* was but half that which went out by the canals.

The following were the *shipments* (not receipts) of flour, wheat and corn from Chicago eastward in the years designated:

Shipments from Chicago.

	Wheat and flour, bus.	Corn, bus.
1856	9,419,365	11,129,668
1857	10,783,292	6.814,615
1858	10,909,243	7.493,212
1859	10.759,359	4,217,654
1860	15,892,857	13,700,113

The shipments from Milwaukie and other lake ports, eastward, were proportionally large. Contrast with the shipments from Chicago alone, as above stated, the following table of *shipments* from New Orleans during the same period:

Shipments from New Orleans.

	Flour, bbls.	Wheat, bus.	Corn, bus.
1856	251,501	1,096,733	2,941,711
1857	428,436	1,353,480	1,034,402
1858	474.906	596,442	1,134,147
1859	133,193	107,031	111,522
1860	80,541	2,189	224,382

The foregoing tables show not only how small a proportion of western grain and flour sought a market by way of the channel of the lower Mississippi and New Orleans, but that this proportion was yearly and rapidly diminishing before the war. The natural tendency of these products is eastward, across the continent, on routes as near as possible to the same parallels of latitude as those on which they are grown. This tendency of trade is pointedly shown by the following tables, for four years, of

Shipments from Cincinnati.

	1857–'8.		1858–'9.	
	Shipped north.	Shipped south.	Shipped north.	Shipped south.
Flour, bbls.	445,650	162,565	544,570	17,569
Wheat, bus.	601,214	30,446	270,531	1,182
Corn, sacks,	17,225	1,927	24,796	3,707

	1859–'60.		1860–'61.	
Flour, bbls.	385,389	92,919	268,033	158,592
Wheat, bus.	310,154	11,341	477,264	47,801

The bulk of this trade took the line of the lakes. Thus strongly does the trade of the west itself appeal for a direct water-line along the shortest route to the seaboard.

Objections to the River and Gulf Route.

Any reflecting mind would have concluded in 1820, when the success of steamboat navigation had been fully demonstrated on western waters, that the course of western trade was thereby determined; that it would never seek artificial lines of transportation where steam navigation could be applied; but would assuredly prefer the course of the Mississippi river to New Orleans and a market. But no sooner was the Erie canal opened in 1825, than produce from the region of the Mississippi began to seek that route to the seaboard. From the country in the region of the lakes, the new route had the advantage of being much shorter and more direct. From the country bordering upon the Ohio river, other considerations gave trade a northeastward direction towards the canal.

It is a well known fact that almost every article of up-country produce is liable to undergo a sweating, souring, and heating process from the warmth and humidity of the climate of the gulf.

The loss in value from this deteriorating cause is sometimes very serious, and always greater or less; being variously estimated at from 5 to 25 per cent. on the value of produce; except when the transit is made in the winter months. Assuming, however, that the average deterioration amounts only to 5 per cent. on bacon, lard, butter, tobacco, and ten per cent. on wheat and flour, we have an average loss of $7 50 per ton on the former class of articles; and of $5 per ton on the latter; a sum which is sufficient to give the control of this trade for most of the year to northern routes. The addition of these items to the comparative estimates of cost of transportation by various routes, given in the report of Mr. Lorraine and the memorial of the Iowa legislature, would make a still greater difference in favor of the Virginia route over that by way of the gulf.

Besides the objection of climate, there are dangers in the navigation of the Mississippi, from snags and other casualties. During the last twenty-five years much has been done to relieve this evil; but the high rates of river steamboat insurance still attest the magnitude of the dangers attending the navigation of the river. Mr. Barrow, in a report to the Senate of the U. S. in 1843, stated the amount of the losses on the Mississippi and its tributaries, from snags alone, at a million of dollars per annum.

The navigation of the gulf of Mexico is subject to the sudden storms and hurricanes incident to the West India climate. In his speech at the Memphis convention in 1845, Mr. Calhoun said on this subject: "With all the advantages possessed by the coasting trade between the gulf and Atlantic, be it ever so well secured against interruption, there is one great objection to which it is liable. The peninsula of Florida projects far south; which makes the voyage from New Orleans and the other ports of the gulf to the southern Atlantic cities, not only long and tedious, but liable to frequent and great accidents in its navigation. A voyage from this place (Memphis), for instance, to Charleston, would be a distance of certainly not less than two thousand five hundred miles, and is subject to as great losses as any voyage of equal extent in any part of the world. It was estimated some dozen years since, that the actual loss between Cuba, the Bahama islands and Florida, was not less than half a million of dollars a year, and it may now, with the great increase of our commerce, be put at not less than a million."

These dangers, coupled with those incident to the navigation of the boisterous coast of the Carolinas, and combined with the great length of the voyage from St. Louis to New York of 4,000 miles, make up a most imposing and formidable array of objections to the river, gulf and seaboard route.

The far-seeing mind of Chief Justice Marshall perceived the effect of these objections as early as 1812. In his report in advocacy of the Virginia canal line, that eminent man said: "The whole of that extensive and fertile country [the valley of the Mississippi], a country increasing in wealth and population with a rapidity which baffles calculation, must make its importations up the Mississippi alone, or through the Atlantic states. When we take into view the certain growth of the country, we can scarcely suppose it possible that any commercial city on the banks of that river [near its mouth*] can keep pace with that growth and furnish a supply equal to the demand. The unfriendliness of the climate to human life will render this disparity between the commercial and agricultural capital still more sensible. It will tend still more to retard a population of that sound commercial character which would render some great city on that majestic river a safe emporium for the western world."

In answer to enquiries addressed by Mr. Cabell, former president of the Virginia canal, to eminent merchants largely engaged in trade, both in Richmond and New Orleans, he received the following replies. Several persons united in saying, that if the Virginia line should bring trade from the west to tide-water at two cents per ton per mile, (which is quadruple the charge at which it will be brought), it was their opinion "that the following articles would pay all the expenses of transportation and net the grower more in Richmond, than if taken to New Orleans free of charge; say tobacco, flour, pork, bacon, lard, butter, cheese, &c., for the following reasons:

"Independent of the freight down the river to New Orleans, these articles are all materially injured, by passing through a warm and humid climate; at New Orleans they have to pay exorbitant rates of drayage, storage, fire insurance and commission, and when shipped from thence to other markets, are subject to a rate of freight at times 50 per cent. higher than from the James river." Genl. Steenbergen, an eminent man of business in the Ohio valley wrote, that "every avenue from the Ohio to the eastern cities at all practicable, and at prices of transportation that can possibly be borne by the shipper, is used in preference to the New Orleans route. It will always be

---

* The context shows that he referred to an importing city near the seaboard.

the case. The climate and dangers of the one, against the certainty and even high prices of the other, will make the inland passage the favorite one."

Of late years, the construction at St. Louis and other points, of great stationary steam elevators for transferring grain from boat to boat, and the employment of floating steam machinery for performing the same office from boat to boat while in motion; and the substitution of barges towed in fleets by steam towboats, for the old plan of carrying the freight on the steamboat, has restored to water transportation an undisputed superiority over railroad carriage and greatly diminished the objections which formerly existed to the route by the lower Mississippi and the gulf. But the injurious effects of the semi-tropical climate upon agricultural produce, the great length of the circuitous gulf route, and the dangers of the gulf and coast navigation, still constitute enduring objections to that route.

DEFECTS OF THE ST. LAWRENCE ROUTE.

The outlet of the St. Lawrence into the ocean is not less than 1000 miles northeast from lake Ontario; about 700 miles of the line consisting of the river itself, and 300 miles of the gulf of St. Lawrence, into which it falls. As to its natural features, this line of navigation, in both of its divisions, was accurately described in 1838 by an eminent English engineer and traveler, Mr. Stevenson, who had made a professional tour of observation in the United States and British America. Mr. Stevenson says of this river:

" Receiving the whole surplus waters of the North American lakes, and the drainage of a great tract of country traversed by the numerous streams which join it in its course to the ocean, the St. Lawrence, as regards the quantity of its discharge, presents abundant advantages for safe and easy navigation. The stream of the upper part of this river, however, is much distorted by numerous expansions and contractions of its banks, and also by declivities or falls in its bed, and clusters of small islands, which render its navigation exceedingly dangerous, and in some places wholly impracticable for all sorts of vessels excepting the Canadian batteaux, which are strong flat-bottomed boats, built expressly for its navigation. In several parts of its course the river expands into extensive lakes ; and in its waters, which are thus distributed over a great surface, numerous shoals occur, among which the ship-channel is generally tortuous and narrow, and only navigable in day-light. In some places again the St. Lawrence forces its way between high banks which encroach on its bed, and leave a comparatively narrow gullet for its passage: and in others it flows over a steep, rugged bottom. These sudden contractions and declivities interrupt the peaceful flow of the stream, and produce *chutes*, as they are called, or rapids, some of which are wholly impassable for vessels of large size, and others can only be navigated in certain states of the tide. The islands, which occur chiefly in the upper part of the river between Montreal and lake Ontario, also disturb the channel, and give rise to rapids which are no less detrimental in a commercial point of view."—[Stevenson's Civil Engineering in America.

The navigation of the river is further embarrassed by the general and strong current of the river, against which ascending vessels can make their way only by the aid of steam tow-boats of the most powerful description to be found in any of the American waters. Since Mr. Stevenson wrote, the rapids and shallows of the river have been flanked by canals, and the falls of the Niagara river have been lapped by the Welland canal—all on the British side The dimensions of these Canadian canals are as follows:

	Length in miles.	Depth in ft.	Size of locks: ft.	Lift ft.	No. locks.
Lachine,	8½	10,	200X45	44¾	5
Beauharnais,	11¼	10,	200X45	82½	9
Cornwall,	11½	10,	200X45	48	7
Farrand's Point,		10,	200X45	4	1
Rapid Plat,	9¾	10,	200X45	11¼	2
Point Iroquois,		10,	200X45	6	1
Gallop's,		10,	200X45	8	2
Welland,	28	10,	150X26½	330	27
	69			534¾	54

The St. Lawrence canals can pass vessels of 800 tons. The Welland canal can pass vessels of 400 tons. These canals connect the lower river and gulf of St. Lawrence with the chain of the great lakes.

Of the gulf of St. Lawrence, Mr. Stevenson gives the following description:

"The navigation of the gulf of St. Lawrence, through which the river discharges itself into the Atlantic, is very hazardous. In addition to the dangers arising from the masses of ice which are constantly to be met with, for nearly one half of the year, it is subject to dense and impenetrable fogs, and its rocky shores and desolate islands, afford neither comfort nor shelter to the shipwrecked mariner. One of the most desolate and dangerous of the islands in the gulf, is Anticosti, which lies exactly opposite the mouth of the St. Lawrence, and is surrounded by reefs of rocks and shoalwater. Two light-houses have been erected on it, and also four houses of shelter, containing large stores of provisions, for the use of those who have the misfortune to be shipwrecked on its inhospitable shores."

In a memorial of citizens of New York, written by De Witt Clinton in 1816, addressed to the legislature of that state, in advocacy of the Erie canal, it is stated that "the St. Lawrence is generally locked by ice seven months in the year, during which time produce lies a dead weight on the hands of the owner." But Mr. Stevenson seems to imply a shorter duration of the period of frost by remarking that it continues "for the space of *at least* five months in the year;" going on further to say: "The rigor of a Canadian winter, covering the face of the country with snow, and congealing every river, lake and harbor, produces a stagnation in trade which cannot fail to have a bad effect on the commerce of the country and the habits of the people, who are compelled to complete their whole business transactions during the summer and autumn months, and remain in a state of comparative indolence during the remainder of the year."

BRITISH PROJECTS IN CANADA.

These difficulties, attending the navigation of the St. Lawrence river and gulf, make that route a feeble competitor for the trade of the great west. Yet British enterprise and capital seem determined to overcome the disadvantages imposed by nature. Not to speak of stupendous railroads constructed from the upper lakes to points on the St. Lawrence, from which they are continued to Portland, Maine, and Boston, Massachusetts, the following plans of water navigation have been projected and are partially in progress.

The principal enterprise is that of a canal on the American side around the falls of Niagara, eight miles in length. It is proposed to make the locks 275 feet long, 46 feet wide, and 13 feet deep on the sills, giving capacity for the passage of vessels of twelve hundred tons.

There are many canals on the Canadian side projected, in progress or completed. The proposed Ottawa ship canal will pass from the easterly side of lake Huron up the French river to lake Nippissingue; from thence by canal across the elevation to Trout lake, at the head of Mattawaco river, and down it to its junction with the Ottawa; following the latter to Montreal. The length of the canal proper is 37¾ miles, and the whole improvement will cost $24,000,000. A recent location makes a line of canal proper 29.32 miles long, and a route of canal and improved river and lake navigation 401½ miles in length from Montreal to lake Huron. It will effect a saving of distance, between Montreal and Chicago, of 842¼ miles over the circuitous route of the great lakes. The locks on this route will be fifty feet wide, 250 feet long and 10 feet on the sills, which will pass vessels of one thousand tons. Lift 665¼ feet.

The Georgian bay and Toronto canal will connect Toronto with lake Huron by a route only 100 miles long, and 470 feet lift of locks. The locks will be 265 feet long, 55 wide, and 12 feet on the sills, costing $22,000,000. By this route the distance between Chicago and Montreal, compared with that by lakes Erie and Ontario, or by the Welland canal, will be 428 miles less.

OBJECTIONS TO THE ROUTE OF THE GREAT LAKES.

The determined enterprise of the British capitalists and colonists who are undertaking the expensive works in Canada, which have just been described, proves two important facts. It proves how much water transportation is still valued and relied on even in latitudes of frost where canals can be used only about 200 days in the year; and *it proves that there is some insuperable objection to navigation on the great lakes, especially those of Erie and Ontario, which it is of great importance to avoid, by shorter lines across the northern peninsula.*

The nature of that objection can be learned from the following facts:

After various unsuccessful experiments, it is perfectly ascertained that ordinary canal boats, such as are in use upon the Ohio and Erie canals, cannot be safely towed upon the stormy surface of the great lakes. The modern barge system cannot, therefore, be applied on the lakes.

The board of the New York state canals, in their report for 1835, set forth the following state of facts:

" The method of towing barges by means of steamboats has been very
3

successfully practiced on the Hudson river; but on the lakes, though a great many steamboats have been in use for several years, the plan has not been adopted, because steamboats cannot manage barges in a storm. . . . . An intelligent gentleman of several years experience in navigating steamboats on lake Ontario, informs us that he considered it impracticable as a regular business for steamboats, to tow vessels with safety on the lakes, unless the vessels were fitted with masts and rigging, and sufficiently manned so as to be conducted by sails in a storm; that storms often rise very suddenly on these lakes, and with such violence as would compel a steamboat to cut loose vessels in tow in order to sustain herself."

These who have not witnessed them can form no adequate idea of the violence of lake storms. The annual damage sustained by the massive masonry of the piers by which the harbors are protected, in which stones weighing upwards of half a ton are sometimes raised from their beds and completely upturned; the range of lofty trees rooted up and thrown upon the bordering shores, and the numerous vessels driven ashore and totally lost or seriously damaged, furnish striking evidences of the power of an agency which nothing can resist. They are even more powerful than the "ground swells" of the ocean near the shore. In all land-locked bodies of water the waves are short and sudden in their movements, proving very destructive to whatever obstacle is opposed to their fury; but there is a characteristic slowness in the long movement of the ocean's swell which, it is generally acknowledged, renders it less destructive to marine works exposed to its action than the waves produced in land-locked lakes or seas.

From Mr. Woodbridge's report to the Senate of the United States in February, 1843, upon the subject of the trade of the lakes, it appears "that from 1834 to 1841, inclusive, the number of wrecks upon lake Michigan amounted to eighty-nine vessels; that those wrecks were accompanied by a destruction of property to the value of $1,052,450; and that one hundred and fifteen lives were sacrificed." The same report makes the disclosure, that during the year 1842 alone, "two steamboats, one ship, and seventeen schooners, were totally lost in the storms on the upper lakes; and that three other steamboats, two brigs, and ten schooners, were driven ashore, accompanied by the probable loss of nearly one half million of value in property, and more than a hundred lives."

From the shallowness of the water upon lake Erie, compared with that upon the other lakes, it is more easily and more permanently affected by frost, its navigation being generally obstructed by ice for some weeks every spring, after that of all the others is open and unimpeded. From the same cause this lake is likewise contradistinguished from all the others, by a slight current constantly setting from the west to east, which, together with the prevailing southwesterly winds, causes the floating ice in spring to drift down to accumulate to a vast extent about the head of the St. Lawrence river, thereby retarding the opening of the navigation at the entrance of the Erie and Welland canals some three weeks beyond the period at which it opens at the port of Erie upon the southern side of the lake.

There is a significant fact disclosed by the last report of the New York canals. For the months of October and December of 1867, the receipts from tolls were about two millions, being a little more than half the receipts for the fiscal year, and more than half the estimated receipts for the next fiscal year. These figures show that the navigation closes just when the demand for transportation is greatest, and the comparative smallness of receipts for the other five months of open navigation shows that the freight which cannot use this canal gets to market over other and much more expensive avenues of transportation.

It is probably owing to this serious disadvantage of the lake route that so little success has attended the various efforts which have been made to institute direct exports from the lakes to Europe. Notwithstanding all these efforts, the following list will show the whole number of vessels that have passed from the lakes to the ocean, from 1846 to 1865 (excepting 1864, 1851, 1852, 1853, and 1849, for which the statistics are not available):

1846	1
1847	2
1848	1
1850	1
1854	1
1855	1
1856	1
1857	2
1858	13
1859	37
1860	39
1861	7
1862	6
1863	36
1865	11
Total	159

When the magnitude of the western lake trade, and when the costliness and perfection of the canals which have been constructed for the passage of ocean shipping, are considered, this must be confessed to be a meagre exhibit, and it affords conclusive proof that *trade avoids the outlet furnished by the St. Lawrence, rather than seeks it.*

For the trade of the vast country lying in the states west and southwest of the lakes, this route does not seem to furnish a cheap outlet. In an able paper on the duty of the Federal government, in connection with the navigation of the Mississippi river and its tributaries, Prof. Sylvester Waterhouse of St. Louis, remarks: "Under all the existing difficulties (of this navigation), the freight of cereals from the upper Mississippi to New York, is far cheaper by way of New Orleans than it is by the lakes and the New York canal. The comparative rates of transportation from Dubuque, Iowa, to New York, are:

Via the lakes,	68 cents per bushel.
Via New Orleans,	38 cents per bushel.

Difference in favor of southern route, 30 cents.

The present cost of shipping grain from Chicago to Cairo *by rail*, and thence *via* New Orleans to New York by water, is no greater than the freight to the same point by way of the lakes. The existing water tariff on wheat in bulk from Chicago to New York, is:—

By the lakes,	44 cents.

From Chicago to Cairo by rail,	20 cents.
From Cairo to New Orleans, by water,	12 cents.
From N. Orleans to New York, by water,	12 cents.

So extreme is the cheapness of river carriage, that the rates of the southern route, increased by 300 miles of costly railroad transit, do not exceed those of the northern line. If we take a point on the Mississippi south of the latitude of Chicago, such as Dubuque, the saving is 30 cents a bushel by the New Orleans route. This gives 38 cents as the cost; and it is believed that after the improvement of the rapids of the Mississippi, and the erection of elevators for the transfer of grain in bulk, the freight of cereals from the upper Mississippi to New York by way of New Orleans, will be reduced to twenty-five cents per bushel."

Such a reduction, and even the present low rates, will powerfully affect the movement of western grain; for even as early as in 1865, out of 48,000,000 bushels of grain shipped to Chicago, 15,000,000 were brought from points on the Mississippi; and it is officially stated that three-fifths of all the wheat received in 1865 at Milwaukie and Chicago, came from the towns on the banks of the Mississippi.

The Virginia Water-line the best Substitute.

The serious disadvantages which have been here detailed attending the navigation of the lakes and the St. Lawrence river and gulf, coupled with the other consideration, that in the event of a war with Great Britain, this important channel of transportation of the produce of the west to the east would be obstructed, have combined to impress upon the public mind of the east the great importance of auxiliary lines of railroad lying wholly within the national jurisdiction.

This well-grounded appreciation of railroads which grew gradually into a railroad mania, operated for several years to turn public attention away for a period from all artificial water-line routes of transportation. But now, it is discovered, after the fullest experiment, that railroads are inadequate to the performance of the immense transportation required, and that they are liable to the popular objection of being in charge of close corporations, and are not, like canals, open to indiscriminate public use at moderate rates of charge.

The Virginia canal, owing to the costliness of the work, did not reach completion before the railroad fever had taken possession of the public; and it has had to wait for its consummation to that returning appreciation, which is now again felt, of cheap water transportation. It offers now a channel of navigation from west to east shorter than any other, cheaper than any other, more expeditious, and more free from all obstructions arising from climate or a public enemy, than all the rest. Its only rivals in capacity, for western trade, are the Mississippi and gulf route on one hand, and the great lake, Erie canal and St. Lawrence river route, on the other. Both of these boundary routes are circuitous, while this central one is direct. Both of the others take American produce out of the Union, in transporting it from one part of the Union to the other, subjecting it to the dangers of war; and while one of them subjects our national products to the damaging effects of a semi-tropical climate, and the hazards of gulf and coast navigation, the other renders it liable to be seized and held for months by the ice, or wrecked and lost by the lake storms.

Emphatically, in the case of the Virginia line, is it true, *in medio tutissimus ibis*. It offers the safest, the shortest, the most central, the cheapest, the most constantly open, and the most available of all the channels of outlet by water for western trade.

The rapid expansion and extension of inland navigation in the central basin of the continent is producing an increase in the quantity of trade demanding outlet to the seaboard, far exceeding the capacity of all existing avenues of outlet to discharge, and imperatively requiring the opening of a new line of direct water navigation to the seaboard equal in capacity to the Erie canal. The extent of this inland navigation will now be displayed in a few paragraphs.

VAST EXTENT OF OUR INLAND NAVIGATION.

The construction of a ship canal less than one mile in length between lakes Traver and Big Stone, in Minnesota, will unite the waters of the river St. Peter's with those of the great Red river of northwest British America. The Red river of the north is navigable for steamboats for seven hundred miles to lake Winnepeg; and from lake Winnepeg, this navigation is extended by the Saskatchawan, seven hundred miles to the base of the Rocky mountains, within a short distance of Frazier's gold diggings. Thus navigation will soon be opened west of the Mississippi from St. Paul, on the Mississippi river, to Frazier's diggings in British Columbia, via the St. Peter's and Red rivers of the north. East of the river, the union of the headwaters of the Wisconsin and Fox rivers in Wisconsin, will make a navigable water route, from the Mississippi to Green bay, on lake Michigan. Further south, one hundred miles of ship canal, from Chicago west to Peoria, with some improvements in the Illinois river, will make another navigable water route for large vessels from the Mississippi to lake Michigan. A canal in Ohio connects Portsmouth on the Ohio river, with Cleveland on lake Erie. Cincinnati on the Ohio river, and Toledo on lake Erie, are connected by the Miami canal. A canal from Toledo to Logansport, Indiana, with the Wabash river, unites the waters of the Ohio river with those of lake Erie at Toledo. Should the wants of commerce require it, these latter canals can be enlarged through Ohio and Indiana, to a capacity for passing steamboats of six hundred tons burden.

The proposed dimensions of the canal above described, as projected for uniting Prairie du Chien on the Mississippi with Green bay on lake Michigan, across the state of Wisconsin, are as follows: The entire improvement will be 295 miles in length, of which 175 miles, chiefly of lake and river navigation, are in use. The locks will be 160 feet long by 35 feet wide. The upper Fox is not yet fully improved, but now passes barges of greater capacity than those of the Erie canal. The dimensions of the water-line through Illinois will be, when the canal is enlarged, length one hundred miles, with locks 350 feet long by 70 feet wide; cost $10,000,000. These two latter works are not antagonistic, and will make a navigable water communication between the great chain of lakes, and upwards of twenty thousand miles of navigable rivers, including the Mississippi and its numerous tributaries, and the Red river of the north and Saskatchawan of British America. These improvements, in connection with the short ship canal, less than a mile long, between lakes Big Stone and Traver, will open steamboat navigation from Chicago or New Orleans to lake Winnepeg, which is seven hundred miles distant from St. Paul. This great sheet of water is as large as lake Ontario, and receives the Saskatchawan river from the west, which itself is navigable seven hundred miles to the Rocky mountains, within a distance of 50 miles from the Frazier's river gold mines. By means of these improvements and the various ship canals proposed or completed between Lake Michigan and the east, steamers from Quebec, New York or New Orleans could be passed to the head-waters of the Missouri, the Yellow Stone and the Saskatchawan, a distance of five thousand miles of inland water navigation. This vast extension of navigation must exert a prodigious influence in stimulating western production, and produce an accumulation of trade requiring the opening of every possible channel of outlet to the seaboard.

The great lakes have a shore line of 3,620 miles on the American side, and 2,629 miles on the side of Canada. Lakes Huron and Superior are navigably connected by a ship canal around the rapids of the St. Marie river, with locks 350 feet long and 50 feet wide, having 12 feet lift.

The present extent of steamboat navigation in the valley of the Mississippi river, is shown by the following table, prepared by Col. Long, of the U. S. army:

EXTENT OF WESTERN STEAM NAVIGATION.

Mississippi and branches.

Mississippi proper	2000
St. Croix	80
St. Peter's	120
Chippeway	70
Black	60
Wisconsin	180
Rock	250
Iowa	110
Cedar	60
Des Moines	250
Illinois	245
Maramec	60
Kaskaskia	150
Big Muddy	5
Obion	60
Forked Deer	195
Big Hatchie	75
St. Francis	300
White	500
Big Black	60
Spring	50
Arkansas	603
Canadian	60
Neosho	60
Yazoo	300
Tallahatchee	300
Tallabusha	100
Big Sunflower	80
Little Sunflower	70
Big Black	150
Cumberland	400
Tennessee	720

Red River and branches.

Red river proper	1500
Wachita	375
Saline	100
Little Missouri	50
Bayou D' Arbourc	60
Bayou Bartholomew	150
Bayou Bœuf	150
Bayou Macon	175

Bayou de Glaze	90
Bayou Carre	140
Bayou Lafourche	60
Bayou Rouze	40
Bayou Plaquemine	12
Bayou Teche	96
Grand River	12
Bayou Sorrelo	12
Bayou Chene	5

Missouri and its branches.

Missouri proper	1500
Yellowstone	300
Platte river	40
Kansas	150
Osage	275
Grand	90

Ohio and its branches.

Ohio proper	1000
Alleghany	200
Monongahela	60
Muskingum	70
Kanawha	65
Big Sandy	50
Scioto	50
Kentucky	62
Salt river	35
Green	150
Barren	30
Wabash	400
Bayou Louis	30
Tensas	150
Lacke Bistenaw	60
Lake Caddo	75
Sulphur Fork	100
Little River	65
Kiamichi	40
Boggy	40
Bayou Pierre	150
Atclafaloya	360

Total......16,674 miles.

Here are nearly seventeen thousand miles of steamboat navigation. It would be a moderate estimate to reckon the slack water navigation of these rivers, for boats other than steamboats, at the same number of miles in addition. And, if we accept the assertion of an eminent European engineer that any stream having a volume of water 19 feet wide and 18 inches deep may be made navigable, and is considered a commercial stream in Europe, then there are still as many miles in addition of navigable water in the great basin; making a total navigation of 50,000 miles for purposes of commerce.

THE BARGE SYSTEM ON THE WESTERN RIVERS. ITS TENDENCY TO DIVERT TRADE FROM THE LAKES TO THE MISSISSIPPI RIVER, AND TO THE OHIO AND VIRGINIA CANAL.

The inadequacy of the present means of outlet for western produce to the seaboard, other than the channel of the Mississippi, is universally acknowledged.* For the sake of cheapness, vast quantities of produce must take the river and gulf route, or not go to market at all. Notwithstanding the objections which exist, and are universally entertained, to that route, its trade is rapidly increasing from the very necessity of the case. Within the last three years it has received so great an impetus, that improvements in the facilities for transferring produce from vessel to vessel, and for towing it upon the water, have become indispensable. The barge system has accordingly been substituted for the old one of placing the produce on large steamboats. Steam tugs of immense strength are employed. They carry no freight. They are simply the motive power. They save delay by taking fuel for the round trip. Landing only at the large cities, they stop barely long enough to attach a loaded barge. By this economy of time and steady movement, they equal the speed of steamboats. The Mohawk made its first trip from St. Louis to New Orleans in six days, with ten barges in tow. The management of the barges is precisely like that of freight cars. The barges are loaded in the absence of the steam

---

*In 1865 Minnesota alone produced 10,000,000 bushels of wheat. Three-fourths of this harvest could have been exported if facilities of cheap transportation had offered sufficient inducement. In 1866, higher prices—which produce the same effect as cheaper freight—led to the exportation of 8,000,000 of bushels. It is such a state of freight charges or of market prices as will leave a profit to the producer which brings out products to market.

tug. The tug arrives, leaves a train of barges, takes another and proceeds. The tug itself is always at work. It does not lie at the levees while the barges are unloading. Its largest stoppage is made for fuel. The power of these boats is enormous. The tugs plying on the Minnesota river sometimes tow 30,000 bushels of wheat apiece. The freight of a single trip would fill 85 railroad cars. Steamboats are obliged to remain in port two or three days for the shipment of freight. The heavy expense which this delay and the necessity of large crews involve, is a grave objection to the old system of transportation. The service of the steam tug requires but few men, and the cost of running is relatively low. The advantages which are claimed for the *barge system* are exhibited by the following table:

	Tugs and Barges.	Steamboats.
Stoppage at intermediate points,	2 hours.	6 hours.
Stoppage at terminal points,	24 "	48 "
Crew,	15 men.	50 "
Tonnage,	25,000 tons.	1,500 tons.
Daily expenses,	$200.	$1,000.
Original cost,	$75,000.	$100,000.

In addition to the ordinary precautions against fire, the barges have this unmistakable advantage over steamboats, they can be cut adrift from each other, and the fire restricted to the narrowest limits. The barges are very strongly built, and have water-tight compartments for the movement of grain in bulk. The transportation of grain from Minnesota to New Orleans by water costs no more than the freightage from the same point by railroad to Chicago. After the erection of a floating elevator at New Orleans, a boat load of grain from St. Paul will not be handled again till it reaches the Crescent city.

The dimensions of the vessels employed on the river between St. Louis and New Orleans are as follows:

Towboats.

Light draft.	Depth of hold.	Breadth.	Length.	Tonnage.
3¼ feet.	5½ feet.	30 ft.	180 ft.	6,500 bus. coal.

Barges.

1¼ feet.	6 feet.	30 ft.	175 ft.	600 tons.
1¼ "	8	34 "	190 "	1,000 "

The towboats have two engines each; the cylinders are 22 inches in diameter, with 20 inch stroke. One towboat will draw eight thousand tons of freight. The time from St. Louis to New Orleans is 6 days down, 10 days back; round trip, on the average, 18 days. "The Mississippi Valley Transportation Company" has 5 towboats and 37 barges. They are crowded with business. They handle as much as 11,000 tons of freight in a week. The business is rapidly and largely developing. The barge system will soon supersede all other methods of transportation on western waters. An indispensable adjunct of it is the steam elevator for transferring grain from vessel to vessel in bulk. The St. Louis elevator cost $450,000, and has a capacity of 1,250,000 bushels. It is able to handle 100,000 bushels a day. It began to receive grain in October 1865. Before the first of January, 1866, its receipts amounted to 600,000 bushels, 200,000 *of which were brought directly from Chicago.* The local receipts at the elevator in 1866 were 1,376,700 bushels. Grain can now be shipped by way of St. Louis and New Orleans to New York and Europe twenty cents a bushel cheaper than it can be carried to the Atlantic by the other existing routes. The effects produced by barge system is thus described by a New Orleans correspondent of the New York *Times:*

NEW ORLEANS, Sunday, April 5, 1868.

CHICAGO AND NEW ORLEANS.

Every one observes how this most enterprising people is prospecting for commercial expansion. Chicago owns about one third of the whole tonnage of the Union. She controls the lakes, and is forcing her way by the St. Lawrence to the ocean. She is penetrating the upper country of the Northwest and intercepting from St. Louis the productions of Iowa and Montana. Recently she has discovered that the Mississippi is the cheapest open way to the markets of the world, so she has sent her commercial explorers to mark her pathway to the ocean by way of New Orleans. The great Illinois Central Railroad has taken hold of the West India trade and offered such inducements to western importers that Havana sends her products by this route instead of by New York. The Texas cattle dealers have adopted this route. Large capital has been put in grain elevators, and western men who are here to conduct the business claim confidently this important commerce. These explorers from the northwest seem delighted with the climate and local attractions of New Orleans, and with a rapid rail time between the snows of the north and the sunny *trottoirs* of

New Orleans, we have crowds of business men, with their families, constantly among us. This has given an impulse to our western trade, and has occasioned considerable investments in city and country real estate.

THE NORTHWEST ON POLITICS.

The giant northwest is, in fact, beginning to perceive and employ its physical ability in the commercial politics of the country. With the conviction that the Mississippi outlet was of indispensable importance, it has decreed that all obstacles to the navigation of that river shall be removed from its sources to its mouth. So the Des Moines canal is under contract. It is to be seven miles long, three hundred feet wide and six feet in depth. The smaller obstructions of the upper river, including the bridge at Rock Island, are to be removed or so modified as no longer to impede navigation. Then the Government has ordered a dredgeboat, costing nearly $400,000, to go to work on the Belize Passes. Besides this, St. Louis is declared a port of entry, and hereafter goods will be imported direct to that city. This will, no doubt, make a great change in the values imported by way of this Custom-house. There are other evidences that this great internal power will make itself felt in the legislation and foreign policy of the government. It is a leviathan, which has only made itself known so far by spouting and an occasional lash of its tail. When its power shall be fully awakened, it will snap the ropes and splinter the lifeboats of the politicians who are after it for its blubber alone. The character of national politics will be fixed by the millions who inhabit the northwest. They are mostly of European origin, believe in the divine right of the majority, think that the minority ought to be hanged for the treason of a difference of opinion. In a word, they have transfused the doctrine of European despotism into the forms of a popular government. Whenever this numerical power shall demonstrate itself, we may anticipate a moral revolution in the political administration of this Democratic Republic.

The employment of the barge system on the Ohio river will, as to all trade accessible to that stream, neutralize the objection to the overland portage from Parkersburg to tide water at Baltimore, by way of the Baltimore and Ohio railroad. At a recent meeting of the Board of Trade of New York, it appeared that transportation by rail to Cincinnati from that city cost 70 cents per hundred; while from Boston and Philadelphia along the Atlantic coast to the mouth of the Chesapeake; thence north to Baltimore; and thence by railroad to Cincinnati, the cost is 40 cents per hundred. The Baltimore Gazette of April 11th, 1868, gives the following table of freight charges respectively from New York and Baltimore to different points in the west on *fourth-class* goods:

	From New York	From Baltimore
To Cincinnati	50	30
" Louisville	66	48
" St. Louis	94	55
" Chicago	55	38
" Indianapolis	53	35

These differences are producing a great diversion to the Baltimore route from the more southern ones, and demonstrate the strong tendency of trade to seek the 'shortest crossing from the west to tide-water.

THE QUESTION OF BACK-LOADING—PRODUCTS OF THE KANAWHA VALLEY.

Transportation by either of the two great routes of circuitous navigation, from the west to the sea, which have been considered, is conducted under the very costly disadvantage of a deficiency of return freights for the boats conveying the trade. The products moved eastward from the west, are gross and bulky, while the freights taken back to the west consist chiefly of articles much lighter and less bulky in proportion to their value. All the statistics of trade between east and west show, that the tonnage moving eastward exceeds by several fold, that moving westward. This condition of trade subjects the boats engaged in it to the necessity of returning westward either wholly or partially empty. In western New York, the deficiency of back-loading thus occasioned, has produced a very great development in the salt manufacture, and swollen that business in that locality probably to the largest salt manufacture in the world.

The reverse state of things now exists in the trade of the Ohio river. A very large portion of the western population derives its coal from the mines on the upper waters of the Ohio. This mineral is bulky in proportion to its value, and boats carrying it down from the region about Pittsburg to the places of consumption, having no sufficient return loading eastward in consequence of there being no outlet of navigation to the seaboard from the upper Ohio, do not return at all, and are broken up for fuel or lumber, and sold at a sacrifice.

The opening of the water-line from the Great Kanawha river, through Virginia to the Atlantic, will correct both of these serious disadvantages incident now to western trade. The boats or barges which shall carry the heavy and bulky farm produce of the far interior to the mouth of Chesapeake bay, will refill in returning with the fine bituminous coals of West Virginia, and carry them back to the very hearths of those western farmers from whose granaries they were loaded for the eastward voyage. The coals of West Virginia would themselves supply all the return tonnage which the boats moving east would require; but in the event of any deficiency in this respect, the Salines of the Kanawha Valley, now producing two millions of bushels of salt per annum, would multiply their production to any possible requirement.

It is well known to geological men that the veins of bituminous coal which pervade the entire western slope of the Appalachian chain of mountains, have their maximum aggregate thickness in the Kanawha Valley.

From a late authentic work on the subject of the Kanawha coals, the following extract is made:

THE GREAT KANAWHA COAL FIELDS.

The coal fields of the Great Kanawha region, in West Virginia, are superior to those of Great Britain or Pennsylvania. They are regarded by eminent geologists *as the finest deposit of coal in the world.* The quality of Kanawha Cannel coal is equal to the best English Cannel; the quality of its bituminous coal is equal to the best found in Pennsylvania; and Kanawha splint coal, for smelting iron ore, is unsurpassed. The veins lie horizontally, and vary from three feet to fifteen feet in thickness; and the aggregate thickness of the various veins in some localities amounts to forty and even fifty feet of solid coal.

The advantages of the Great Kanawha Coal Fields over those near Pittsburg may be summed up as follows:

1. The Kanawha Coal Fields contain as good bituminous coal as the best found on the Monongahela and Youghiogheny, and, in addition thereto, large deposits of *Cannel coal*, equal in quality to the best English Cannel— none of which is found in the Monongahela coal fields.

2. The veins of coal are thicker and more numerous on the Kanawha than on the Monongahela. Veins of splint and bituminous coal on the Kanawha are from four feet to fifteen feet thick, and the Cannel from thirty inches to five feet thick.

3. Coal lands on the Monongahela and Youghiogheny sell for $300 and $400 per acre, whilst better coal lands on the Kanawha can now be purchased from $10 to $20 per acre.

4. The Kanawha Coal Fields are 230 miles nearer to Cincinnati and the southwest cities than the Monongahela coal fields are. This gives to Kanawha

coal an advantage of *at least one cent per bushel in cost of transportation* to such markets over the Monongahela and Youghiogheny coal. (See map.)

5. The navigation of the Ohio at Point Pleasant is greatly better than it is at Pittsburg; therefore, Kanawha coal can be more frequently shipped from Point Pleasant than Monongahela coal can from Pittsburg.

6. The navigation of the Kanawha and Lower Ohio is not interrupted by ice to the extent that the navigation of the Monongahela and Upper Ohio is, as New River, the chief tributary of the Kanawha, rises in North Carolina—whilst the Alleghany (which, with the Monongahela, forms the Ohio), rises near Lake Erie. This gives to the Ohio River at Point Pleasant an advantage of two weeks, and more every winter over the Ohio at Pittsburg—and at a time when fuel is most needed in Cincinnati and Louisville.

7. The Kanawha Coal Fields are situated on what must be, in time, a great highway for the trade and travel of the Mississippi Valley to the Atlantic seaboard. The vast and rapidly increasing trade of the Great West is seeking new routes for transit to the cities of the seacoast; and the route through the Kanawha valley has advantages over all others in *shortness of distance, grade of road and mildness of climate.*

Coals for the Seaboard Cities and Factories.

The coals of the Kanawha region are now shipped around by way of New Orleans and the Gulf to New York, at a profit to the miner and dealer. The quality of the cannel coals of West Virginia is fully equal to that of the coals of England and Nova Scotia imported into New York. It has become of vital importance to the manufacturing interests of the seaboard cities to obtain adequate supplies of the best qualities of bituminous coals from shorter distances than those from which they are now derived, and at cheaper rates. The most intelligent manufacturers, and dealers in coal, of New York and the eastern cities, recognize the necessity of a resort to the excellent cannel and bituminous coals of the Kanawha, Coal, Guyandotte and Sandy rivers of West Virginia for fuel;—a fact which is fully established by the shipments that are now making of the coals of that region by the roundabout route of New Orleans to the Atlantic seaboard.

The opening of the Virginia canal will finally settle the question of an adequate coal supply for the eastern cities, and forever relieve the apprehension and scarcity now felt by eastern manufacturers on that vital subject. Valuable as this water-line will be to the West, as shown in these pages, its importance is doubled by the fact that the work is vital to the success of the manufacturing system of the East, as a means of supplying the best coals of the continent from the nearest mines by the most direct navigation and at the cheapest rates.

DUTY OF CONGRESS ON THE SUBJECT OF INLAND NAVIGATION.

"The invention of Fulton has, in reality for all practical purposes, converted the Mississippi, with all its great tributaries,into an *inland sea*. Regarding it as such, I am prepared to place it on the same footing with the gulf and Atlantic coasts, the Chesapeake and Delaware bays, and the lakes, in reference to the superintendence of the general government over its navigation. It is manifest that it is far beyond the power of individuals or of separate states to supervise it, as there are eighteen states, including Texas and the territories—more than half the Union—which lie within the valley of the Mississippi or border on its navigable tributaries." (J. C. Calhoun in Memphis Convention of 1845.)

Pertinent to this question of congressional duty, with reference to the western rivers, there is an important provision in that great organic law of the northwest, the Ordinance of 1787. By that law, enacted by congress for the government of the territory of the United States northwest of the Ohio river, it is declared that "the navigable waters leading into the Mississippi and St. Lawrence, and the *carrying places between the same*, shall be common highways and forever free, as well to the inhabitants of the said territories, as to the citizens of the United States, and those of other states that may be admitted into the Confederacy, without any tax, impost, or duty therefor." It may be asked, how can the people of the United States at large enjoy the benefits of this common right, unless they have avenues of access opened to them by a competent power; and how can the people of the country bordering those streams enjoy the benefit of their navigation, if that inland navigation be not connected with the seaboard, by direct lines of artificial navigation, opened by competent authority? This Ordinance is in the nature of a compact between the general government and the people of the states, and it reserves certain rights, and imposes certain duties, in which all citizens of the United States are interested. It is a part of the fundamental law of the land. Reserving the rivers *as common highways for all*, it divests all the states, and each particular state, of any jurisdiction over them; and gives congress full power to extend their advantages to every citizen of the Union.

Having guarantied to all the people the navigation of these rivers forever, the United States is bound to open avenues to them from all directions, and keep them in a condition to be freely navigated and fully enjoyed. But how can an inland navigation be fully enjoyed, if congress shall supply no direct and convenient outlet to the seaboard and to the markets of the world?

It is now conceded that congress has power, as proprietor of the public lands, to do what any prudent land owner may do for the enhancement of the value of his patrimony, and can lawfully appropriate part of its lands in aid of public works which would commensurately enhance the lands retained. If this be so, what method could be conceived of that would more certainly enhance the value of every acre of public lands in the west, than the opening of another canal of the capacity of the Erie, on a more central, more southern, and shorter route?

The attentive reader of these pages cannot fail to have arrived at the conviction, that water navigation affords greater advantages to greater numbers of people, at lower rates, and for far more numerous tons of produce than railroad transportation. Yet railroads have received nearly all the bounties which Congress has been willing to bestow upon public roads.

The commissioner of the General Land Office, in his report for 1865 (pp. 34–5) gives the following information:

"The immense railroad grants [of land by Congress] embrace, by estimate, the quantity of one hundred and twenty-five millions of acres; exceeding by eight millions of acres the aggregate area of the States of Maine, New Hampshire, Vermont, Connecticut, New York, New Jersey, Pennsylvania, Delaware, and Maryland. These enormous grants are within about one-fourth of being twice the united area of England, Scotland, Wales, Ireland, Guernsey, Jersey, the Isle of Man, and islands of the British seas, and less than a tenth of being equal to the French empire proper, with its 89 departments and its 37,510 communes.

"Why is it that the Congress of the United States, as the national trustee, charged under the constitution with the disposal of the public lands, have made grants on such a stupendous scale as this? The answer is found not merely in the indemnifying principle of duplicating the reserved sections, but in the higher purpose of opening speedy communication by the iron railway across the continent to unite the great industrial interests of the Atlantic slope, the valley of the Mississippi, and the declivity from the Rocky mountains to the Pacific."

Does not a line of direct eastward navigation, promising similar results to those which followed the opening of the Erie canal, present a very strong claim upon the bounty of Congress?

A CROWNING ACT OF RECONSTRUCTION.

The effect upon public opinion in the southern states, of liberal grants of aid by congress in behalf of public works of national importance within their borders, would be unspeakably happy. And no act of such assistance would be more gratefully received, or be more beneficial in result, than a donation of lands and loan of bonds in behalf of so important an enterprise as the completion of the Virginia water-line. Such an act, giving earnest of a broad beneficent policy, would exert as great an influence in securing thorough and permanent reconstruction, as any measure that could be adopted by the Federal power. It would completely identify Virginia with the great West, and utterly and finally obliterate every sentiment and trace of sectional alienation. It would give that bounding prosperity to the state which brings solace for every grievance and sweeps away every remnant of the poverty and privation which are the sure nurses of disaffection and resentment. The completion of a great line of trade across the territory of Virginia would bind that great leading southern state to the bosom of the Union by the strong ties of prosperous commerce, and hold her in indissoluble allegiance for all time to come.

The bestowal of such a bounty at a period of so much need as the present upon a commonwealth which, at a former era of the national history, made notable sacrifices in behalf of the national cause, would be a requital not inappropriate, and would do as much to restore an era of good feeling and sterling loyalty as any measure that could be taken to that end.*

OFFICIAL HISTORY AND DESCRIPTION OF THE VIRGINIA CANAL.

In pursuance of suggestions proceeding from the west, Mr. Charles S. Carrington, president of the James River and Kanawha

---

* In compiling the foregoing pages, much information has been drawn from the admirable Report of Mr. Elmore H. Walker on the Trade and Commerce of Buffalo, and from writings of Professor Sylvester Waterhouse of St. Louis, and Mr. Thos. M. Monroe of Dubuque.

Company, has requested Mr. Edward Lorraine, the able Chief Engineer of the works of that company, to prepare a report of leading facts relating to the important canal with which he is connected. This task has been very ably and satisfactorily performed by that competent officer, in the following interesting and instructive paper:

ERRATA:—Page 45, line 8, "*Southern*" should be "*Northern*;" also, page 47, second line, "*See map*," should have been omitted.

OFFICE OF THE JAMES RIVER AND KANAWHA COMPANY, }
Richmond, June 10th, 1868. }
CHARLES S. CARRINGTON, ESQ.

President of the James River and Kanawha Company:

SIR:—At your request, and with a view of furnishing reliable information to persons who feel interested in the completion of the James River and Kanawha Canal, and of supplying data by which the superiority of this route over all others as a means of transportation of western products to the Atlantic seaboard may be demonstrated, I have prepared the following historical and statistical sketch of this improvement, to which I have added some suggestions as to the best plan for its completion, with estimates of its probable cost. I propose simply to collect together all the interesting statistics which now lie scattered through a vast number of reports and documents, and combine them in one comprehensive paper, which may serve as a text book and magazine of facts, for those seeking information on this subject.

HISTORY OF THE JAMES RIVER AND KANAWHA CANAL.

An act for clearing and improving the navigation of James river was passed by the Legislature of Virginia on the 5th of January, 1785. By this act the first or old James river company was incorporated. They were required to make the river navigable for vessels drawing one foot water at least, from the highest place practicable to the great falls beginning at Westham, and from said falls to make such canal or canals with sufficient locks, as would open navigation to tide-water. This organization continued until the 17th day of February, 1820, on which day the Legislature passed an act to amend the "Act for clearing and improving the navigation of James river, and for uniting the eastern and western waters, by the James and Kanawha rivers." By this act the rights and interests of the James River Company were transferred to the commonwealth, and by an act passed February 24th, 1823, all the rights, powers, duties and privileges of the president and directors were conferred on the Board of Public Works, whose transactions were to be still in the name of the "James River Company." This organization continued until the year 1835.

The old James River Company constructed a canal around the falls of James river, extending from the city of Richmond to Westham, a distance of about seven miles, and improved the bed of the river by sluices as high up as Buchanan.

The *second* James River Company, on state account, enlarged and reconstructed the former canal from Richmond to Westham, and extended the same to Maiden's Adventure in Goochland county, a distance of 27 miles; constructed a canal through the Blue Ridge, seven and a half miles long; constructed a turnpike road from Covington to the mouth of Big Sandy river, two hundred and eighty miles long; and improved the Kanawha river by wing dams and sluices from Charleston to its mouth, a distance of 58 miles.

The *James River and Kanawha Company* was incorporated March 16th, 1832, and organized May 25th, 1835. By the charter the whole interest of the commonwealth in the works and property of the then existing James River Company was transferred to the James River and Kanawha Company; the state being interested in the latter to the extent of three-fifths of its capital stock, and individuals and corporations to the extent of the remaining two-fifths.

The works of the James River Company were valued at one million dollars, the state receiving a credit for that amount in part of her subscription to the capital stock of the James River and Kanawha Company. The new company, moreover, was charged with the payment of the annuity of $21,000 forever to the stockholders of the old James River Company; and as this sum is equivalent to a principal of $350,000, at six per cent. interest, it will be seen that the present company took the old works at the price of $1,350,000.

The construction of the new canal from Richmond to Lynchburg was commenced in 1836, and the work was completed about the first of December, 1840.

In that time the work of construction of the second division of the canal above Lynchburg, was commenced, and prosecuted up to the year 1842, when for want of funds it was abandoned. On the 1st of March, 1847, an appropriation of $1,246,000 was made by the Legislature for the purpose of completing the unfinished work between Lynchburg and North river, and the extension and completion of the canal to Buchanan.

The work was commenced in July, 1847, and completed in November, 1851.

Fifteen miles of the 3rd division of the canal, next above Buchanan, was put under contract in August, 1853, but for want of funds the work was suspended in the fall of 1856. The work done on this portion of the line consisted chiefly of stone locks, acqueducts and tunnelling.

The original capital of the company was five million dollars, of which the state paid one million in old works, and of the private subscription there proved to be insolvent $73,336, leaving $3,926,664 as the actual available cash capital. All beyond the capital thus realized, has been money either borrowed directly from the state treasury or on bonds guaranteed by the state, on which the company has been required to pay interest from the day it was received, before it was expended, and of course long before it began to yield any return.

The actual cost of construction of the James River and Kanawha Canal, including the incomplete works above Buchanan, has been as follows:

Dock and tide-water connection,	$ 851,312
First division, Richmond to Lynchburg,	5,837,628
South-side connections,	162,685
Rivanna connection,	115.043
Second division, Lynchburg to Buchanan,	2,422,556
North river improvement,	536,551
Third division, work done,	511,094
Total,	$10,436,869

The money expended in the construction of works, over and above the amount of the cash capital, which, as stated, was borrowed directly or indirectly from the state, together with the accrued interest, amounted in the year 1860 to about $7,200,000, which sum was assumed as the debt due by the company to the state.

Under this heavy load of debt, with its whole property under a lien to the state, it was impossible for the company to make any further progress with its works.

To relieve the company from its embarrassment and to enable it to complete the canal to Covington, the Legislature, on the 23rd of March, 1860, passed an "act to amend the charter of the James River and Kanawha Company," by which the capital stock of the company was increased to twelve million four hundred thousand dollars, in shares of one hundred dollars each, and the Board of Public Works was directed to subscribe on behalf of the commonwealth, in addition to the shares now owned by the state in said company, for seventy-four thousand shares of said capital stock, which shall be declared by said company a six per cent. preferred stock, on which six dollars per share shall be paid to the holders thereof, before any dividend shall be paid on other stock of said company; whereof seventy-two thousand shares shall be taken in full satisfaction of the debt now due from the said company to the state, and for the assumption by the state of the debt for which the state is bound as the surety for said company, and the annuity to the old James River Company; and for the residue of two thousand shares, the bonds of the state for the aggregate amount of two hundred thousand dollars are to be delivered to the company, to be applied to the extinguishment of the floating debt of the company. The company was also authorized to borrow money at a rate of interest not exceeding seven per cent. per annum, and not exceeding two million five hundred thousand dollars, for the purpose of completing the canal to Covington. The company being thus relieved of its indebtedness to the state and released from the lien upon its property, was placed in a condition by which it was hoped and believed it would be enabled to borrow money sufficient to complete the canal to Covington.

About this time a French gentleman, representing a company of European capitalists, and vouched for by the French consul in Richmond, proposed to enter into an engagement for completing the canal to the Ohio river on an enlarged scale. His propositions, after protracted consideration, were acceded to by the company, and the requisite legislation was obtained from the state. The civil war intervened to prevent the execution of the provisions of this engagement, which was finally abandoned in the spring of 1867.

On the first March, 1867, the Legislature of Virginia passed an act authorizing the James River and Kanawha Company "to borrow the sum of seven hundred and fifty thousand dollars to be applied to paying off the floating debt of the company, putting and keeping its present works in repair, and to give a mortgage on the property, franchises and nett revenues of the company, for the purpose of securing such loan."

A committee of the stockholders at their called meeting in March, 1867, reported the floating debt of the company to be about $622,480. For the purpose of liquidating this debt, the Board of Directors have issued the six per cent. bonds of the company, payable in twenty years from their date, and have executed a mortgage conveying the property, franchises and nett revenues of the company in trust to secure the said bonds.

Up to this time about $410,000 of the floating debt of the company has been paid in cash or funded in the mortgage bonds, leaving about $240,000 still to be adjusted, and it is hoped that in a short time the whole debt will be liquidated.

Having thus briefly related the history, affairs and condition of the company up to the present time; I now proceed to give

A Description of the Virginia Water-Line.

The Virginia water-line extends from the capes of Virginia to the Ohio river, a distance of 636 miles, and consists of

I.

The James river from its mouth to the head of navigation at the city of Richmond, a distance of 151 miles; and

II.

The James River and Kanawha improvement, extending from the city of Richmond to Point Pleasant, at the mouth of the Kanawha river, a distance of 485 miles.

James river is navigable for ships of one thousand tons burden, drawing sixteen feet, from its mouth to City Point, 36 miles below Richmond, and at an inconsiderable expense, by dredging the channel, can be excavated so as to admit vessels of that draught up to the wharves of the city.

The James River and Kanawha improvement, for the purpose of description, will be divided into

1st. The Richmond dock and tide-water connection,	1.00 mile.
2nd. The first division of the canal, extending from Richmond to Lynchburg,	146.50 "
3rd. The second division of the canal, extending from Lynchburg to Buchanan,	50.00 "
4th. The third division of the canal, extending from Buchanan to Covington,	47.00 "
5th. The fourth division of the canal, extending from Covington to the Greenbrier river,	33.33 "
6th. The Greenbrier and New rivers to Lyken's shoals on the Kanawha,	123.21 "
7th. The Kanawha river from Lyken's shoals to the Ohio river,	85.12 "

First. The Richmond Dock and Tide-water connection. By means of this improvement vessels ascend from the river into the dock, where they are met by canal boats which descend from the basin at the terminus of the canal, and lie alongside the vessels for the purpose of exchanging cargoes; or the canal boats can descend to the river, and without breaking bulk, be towed to City Point or to Norfolk.

Vessels enter the dock by means of a shiplock, which is founded upon solid rock, and built of the most substantial cut granite. It is 180 feet long between the gates, 35 feet wide, has a lift of 15 feet, and has 16 feet water on the mitre sill. It will pass vessels of 500 tons.

The dock is 4,100 feet long from the shiplock to 17th street, and has a continuous wharf, protected by a granite wall, for its whole length on the north side, and for about 1,000 feet on the south side. The depth is from 11 to 15 feet, and the average width 100 feet. Above 17th street is a continuation called "the upper dock," which is also surrounded by a substantial granite wall, and is made accessible to small class vessels by means of a pivot bridge across the line of 17th street extended. This upper portion is 800 feet long and 200 feet wide. At its upper extremity is the depot of the Richmond and Danville railroad.

The dock is connected with the basin by means of five locks, having an aggregate lift of 69 feet.

These locks are built of hewn granite, and with the shiplock, in their style and finish, will compare favorably with any similar works in this country.

The total cost of the dock and tide-water connection has been $851,312. It was completed in 1854.

Second. The first division of the canal, extending from the basin in Richmond to the city of Lynchburg, comprising 137¾ miles of canal, and 8¾ miles of slack-water navigation.

The trunk of the canal is 30 feet wide at the bottom and 50 feet wide at the water line, and was originally cut to a depth of five feet. The towpath is 12 feet wide and the berm bank 8 feet.

The locks are 100 feet long between the gates and 15 feet wide in the chamber. The total lockage from the basin in Richmond to Lynchburg, is 429 feet. The works of art on the first division consist of 52 lift locks having a total lift of 429 feet; 6 guard locks; 2 accommodation locks; 3 principal dams across James river, affording slack-water navigation; 9 other dams across James river, or to islands in the river, which serve as feeders to the canal, or for connection with the south side of the river; 11 aqueducts, three of which have wooden trunks and the remainder are of cut stone;

191 culverts; 133 farm and road bridges over the canal, and 3 towpath bridges. Of the locks 22 are built of cut stone and the remainder of rubble masonry, faced with timber and plank. This division of the canal has cost $5,837,628 or $39,982 per mile.

On the first division are works connecting the canal with the south side of James river, usually called the "southside connections." These works are a dam and an outlet lock at Cartersville, and three bridges; one at New Canton, one at Hardwicksville, and one at Bent Creek. The wooden superstructures of the bridges were burned during the late war. They were built upon cut stone abutments and piers which remain uninjured. The total cost of the southside connections has been $162,685.

There is also a connection on the north side of the river with the improvement of the Rivanna river, an important tributary to the canal, which has cost the James River and Kanawha Company the sum of $115,043.

Third. The second division of the canal extends from the city of Lynchburg to the town of Buchanan, a distance of 50 miles, and consists of 22 miles of canal, and 28 miles of slack water navigation. The principal works of art on this division are:

38 locks, having a total lift of 299 feet, built with a few exceptions of cut stone; 4 stone dams and 7 timber dams, across James river; one aqueduct of 50 feet span; 8 culverts; 48 square drains; 17 towpath bridges and two farm bridges. It was completed in the year 1850, and has cost $2,422,556, or $48,451 per mile.

Connected with the second division is the *North river improvement,* extending from the mouth of North river to the town of Lexington, a distance of 19¾ miles. Of this improvement 10 miles are canal and 9¾ miles are slack water navigation. The principal works of art are: 22 locks, all of rubble masonry, and of the same size as those on the main line of the canal, and having a total lift of 188 feet; 9 stone dams and one timber dam across North river, and 4 aqueducts. This work was completed in the year 1860, and cost $536,551.

Fourth. The third division of the canal follows the valley of the James and Jackson rivers from Buchanan to Covington, a distance of 47 miles.

This division has been definitively located, and the first 15 miles above Buchanan was put under contract in the year 1853, but for the want of funds the work was suspended in 1856.

Forty-one miles are canal, and six miles slack water navigation. The total lockage 436¾ feet.

The principal mechanical structures are 36 lift-locks, two guard locks, one guard and lift-lock, five aqueducts across James river, each about 320 feet long, 3 aqueducts of 50 feet span, and 3 dams across James river. There are also the Marshall tunnel, 1900 feet long, and the Mason tunnel, 198 feet long, by means of which $5\frac{5}{8}$ miles of distance are saved.

Of this work there are nearly completed ten lift-locks, and the abutments and piers of three of the aqueducts across James river. The foundations of two of the dams, up to the surface of low water, have been put in; about 800 feet of the Marshall tunnel has been excavated, and the Mason tunnel is completed. The mechanical work on this division is executed in the best style, and of the most substantial materials, all of the structures being built of hewn limestone, laid with hydraulic cement.

Fifth. The fourth division of the canal, extending from the town of Covington to the Greenbrier river, a distance of $33\frac{1}{4}$ miles.

At Covington the canal crosses Jackson river by an aqueduct, and follows the valley of Dunlap's creek to Crow's tavern, at the base of the Alleghany mountains; a distance of $17\frac{1}{2}$ miles.

At Crow's the line of canal leaves the valley of Dunlap's creek, and following the bed of Fork run, ascends the eastern side of the Alleghany mountain, by a series of locks and dams, to the summit.

The distance from Covington to the eastern entrance of the Alleghany tunnel is 20.7 miles, and the total lockage is 675 feet.

The summit level is $4\frac{1}{2}$ miles long, 1921 feet above tide-water, and pierces the Alleghany mountain by a tunnel $2\frac{6}{10}$ miles long.

Emerging from the western side of the mountain the canal descends by the vallies of Tuckahoe and Howard's creeks, 241 feet, in a distance of ten miles to the Greenbrier river.

The summit level, and the portion of the canal on each side of it between Dunlap's creek and the Greenbrier river, a distance of $15\frac{1}{2}$ miles, will be supplied with water chiefly from Anthony's creek. Upon this creek a reservoir is to be made, covering 2,753 acres of land, and having an average depth of 60 feet, from which the water will be conducted by a feeder canal, about 9 miles long, to the summit level.

Sixth. The Greenbrier and New rivers, from the mouth of Howard's creek to Lyken's shoals on the Kanawha, a distance of 123 miles.

From the mouth of Howard's creek to the Ohio river, the character of the improvement will be changed. The line that we have been heretofore occupied with from Richmond to the Greenbrier river is to consist of a canal. The line down the Greenbrier, New and Kanawha rivers, will consist of a slack-water and sluice improvement of those rivers for *steamboat navigation*, and the mouth of Howard's creek, or what is known as "Greenbrier bridge," will be either the point of transhipment from steamboats and barges to canal boats, or the point where canal boats having been towed up by steamboats will change *steam power for horse power*, and *vice versa*.

1st. Greenbrier river from Greenbrier bridge to New river, a distance of 49.62 miles. Lockage 316 feet.

2nd. New river to Lyken's shoals on the Kanawha, a distance of 73.59 miles. Lockage 766 feet.

The surveys of the Greenbrier and New rivers have not been so elaborate nor so exact as those of other parts of the line, but they have been sufficient to obtain a correct profile, and the general character of the beds of the streams, and to establish beyond any doubt the practicability of their improvement. Of the practicability of their improvement we may feel well assured by the concurrent opinions of Benjamin Wright, Edward H. Gill and Charles B. Fisk, three eminent, practical hydraulic engineers. Judge Wright, after acquiring practical experience and high reputation on the Erie canal, was selected as the first chief engineer of the James River and Kanawha Company. In his letter to the board of directors, published in the 7th annual report, page 73, he says: "From the facts disclosed by the survey on the lines of the Greenbrier and New rivers, I am satisfied that the difficulties of improving these rivers have heretofore been overrated, and that the plans proposed for that purpose are both practical and expedient."

Mr. Fisk, the late eminent chief engineer of the Chesapeake and Ohio canal, has also personally examined the Greenbrier and New rivers, and approved of the proposed plan for their improvement.

Mr. Gill, who made the survey of these rivers, in his report of the survey, published in the 7th annual report, page 65, says: "Nature has with a prolific hand, within these rockbound shores, furnished all the elements for the construction of a cheap and permanent improvement, consisting of locks and dams, sites for the erection of which, of the most desirable description, and materials of the best quality for their construction, are distributed along the entire route in profusion.

"And feeling confident that the latter description of improvement is the most permanent and economical that can be adopted on this stream, I recommend it."

I have estimated this section of the improvement from Mr. Gill's notes of the width and fall of the rivers, and have provided for locks and dams built of stone, and adapted to steamers of 350 tons.

Seventh. *The Kanawha river*, from Lyken's shoals to its mouth, a distance of 85 miles, fall 76½ feet.

Various plans have been recommended for the improvement of the Kanawha; but as the improvement by sluices has been proved to be practicable, is by far the cheapest, the least liable to accidents from freshes, and presents the advantages of an open unobstructed navigation, I have adopted it as the basis of my estimate.

PRACTICABILITY OF THE ROUTE.

Before presenting my estimates of its cost, it will be proper to express some views in regard to the practicability of the water-line. The only points, I believe, about which any doubts have been expressed as to the practicability of the route, have been the improvement of New river and the summit level. As to New river, I have already given the testimony and opinion of three practical hydraulic engineers, and I do not think that I can add anything that can strengthen, nor do I think that the crude off-hand, superficial views of unprofessional persons, ought to weaken the confidence that the opinions of these eminent engineers should impart to the public. I will therefore pass on to the summit level.

The only doubts, I believe, that have been expressed in regard to the practicability of this part of the line, have been as to the sufficiency of the supply of water; and as but few persons have taken the trouble to inform themselves on this subject, it will be proper here to explain more fully the plan by which it is proposed to supply the summit level with water, and to demonstrate its practicability and its sufficiency.

It is proposed to supply the summit level with water from Anthony's creek, a tributary of the Greenbrier. Where that stream passes through the Greenbrier mountain there is a narrow defile, which has been selected as a site for a dam or mound, which when erected will arrest the water that flows down the creek and convert the valley above into a reservoir or lake. This reservoir will be nine miles long, will have an average width of half a mile, a superficial area of two thousand seven hundred and fifty-three acres, and a mean depth of sixty feet. The mound will be one hundred and twenty-six feet high and three hundred and ninety-five feet long. The reservoir will contain 178,000,000 cubic yards of water, which was ascertained by an accurate survey of its superficial area; after which cross-sections of its depth were taken at every considerable variation in the ground, with the angles of the hillside at every station of 100 feet. The reservoir was thus divided into a number of fields, the superficial and cubic contents of which were separately calculated. In order to utilize this immense body of water, it will be necessary that the mountain ridge that separates the southern border of the lake from the valley of Howard's creek, shall be pierced by a tunnel two and a half miles long. The level of the bottom of this tunnel will be thirty feet below the surface of the water in the lake. It passes for its entire length through a black slate rock of easy excavation, and as it will be necessary to be made only just large enough to be advantageously worked, it cannot be considered an obstacle of any serious importance. After passing through this tunnel the water from the reservoir will flow down the bed of Dry creek, and at the narrow gorge, where it enters into the valley of the North fork of Howard's creek, a dam 300 feet long and 20 feet high, will be constructed to stop the water, and turn it through a tunnel two hundred yards long into the valley of the Middle fork of Howard's creek, after which it will be conducted by a feeder canal two and eight-tenths of a mile long to the summit level.

It will be observed that as this feeder tunnel is located on a level thirty feet below the surface of the lake, it is proposed to use only the upper thirty feet of the water, which will be the quantity that will be available for feeding purposes, and which has been ascertained to be 109,189,130 cubic yards.

The annual quantity of water discharged by Anthony's creek, has been ascertained by daily gauges of the creek for a whole year, and is stated in the following

Table

Of the Quantity of Water Discharged by Anthony's Creek in one Year.

Months.	Cubic Yards of Water Discharged.
January	11.649.673
February	40.628.408
March	38.455.285
April	45.333.023
May	13.262.939
June	19.208.005
July	4.586.482
August	7.071.220
September	1.194.709
October	780.491
November	6.963.657
December	21.393.063
Total	210.526.955 per annum.
Average discharge per diem	576.786 cubic yards.

These gauges of the creek were taken during the last half of the year 1851, and the first half of the year 1852, during which time the quantity of rain, as ascertained by the rain gauges, which were kept in that vicinity, was 34¼ inches. The average downfall of that year and the preceding four years, was 36.4 inches, and the maximum in 1847-48, was 39.5 inches. So the quantity of rain that fell during the year the creek was gauged, was considerably below the average, and we will therefore be within the mark if we assume 576,786 cubic yards as the average daily supply.

I consider this the actual available supply from the creek, and make no deduction for evaporation or filtration from the reservoir, because the surface of ground covered by the reservoir is greater than the surface of the reservoir, and was subject to evaporation while the gauges of the creek were being taken, and the flow of the creek was diminished by the quantity evaporated from that surface, and there could be no leakage, filtration or absorption in the reservoir, except through the mound, because after the water has passed through and saturated the thin overlying stratum of soil, it would reach the impenetrable rock, and there it would have to stop; there could be no further absorption or filtration. The filtration through the mound, if it was properly made and puddled, would be so slight as to be unworthy of notice. But after the water has left the reservoir it will pass over six miles of branch and canal, from which there would be evaporation and filtration. I will then allow that this six miles of feeder will lose the whole of its prism of water once in every fifteen days, and assuming its area of cross section at 64 square feet, estimate the quantity thus lost at 5,006 cubic yards per diem, which deducted from 576.786 cubic yards, will leave 571,780 cubic yards as the actual supply for feeding the canal.

As doubts had been suggested as to the adaptation of this valley for the purposes of a reservoir, and vague surmises expressed as to fissures and caverns in the sides of the mountain through which the water would leak out, an eminent practical geologist was employed to make an examination of the geological structure of the site of this reservoir, who reported that "if the engineers had the choice of the rocks of this region, it would be difficult to show how they could make a better disposition of them;" and he also expressed the opinion that the building a dam across the gorge of the mountain would reproduce the conditions that once existed, as there was abundant evidence to prove that the valley had been once occupied by a lake, which had subsequently, by a disruption of the mountain, escaped through the gorge.

Having now ascertained the quantity of water afforded by the creek, and the fact that it can be made available, the next step is to determine the quantity that will be needed for the use of the canal, and to see whether the supply will be equal to the demand.

The whole length of the canal to be supplied entirely by this reservoir is that portion between the point on the eastern side of the summit where Dunlap's creek is taken in as a feeder, and the point on the western side of the summit where Howard's creek is taken in as a feeder, a distance of about nine miles.

After the prism of the canal shall have been filled, the yearly supply which will be demanded from the reservoir will be a quantity sufficient to supply the loss by leakage through the locks, and filtration and evaporation from the canal, and the quantity consumed in the passage of the boats through the locks at the summit level. In experiments made by Mr. Fisk on the Chesapeake and Ohio canal, the loss by leakage through the locks, which are 100 feet long and 15 feet wide, amounted to 62 cubic feet per minute, and the monthly loss on the same canal from evaporation and filtration, was about twice the quantity of water contained in it. As the locks proposed for the summit level of our canal will be at least 120 feet long by 20 wide, the proportional quantity to be allowed for leakage through them would be about 100 cubic feet per minute, and the loss by evaporation and filtration from a canal 70 feet wide and 7 feet deep, would be 96 cubic feet per minute per mile. That portion of the canal occupied by the tunnel, being through solid rock, will be subject to no more loss by leakage and evaporation than will be supplied by percolation through the roof and sides of the tunnel, and is therefore excluded from this calculation; leaving the entire length of the canal subject to filtration and evaporation six and a half miles.

The total loss then by leakage, filtration and evaporation would be 724 cubic feet per minute, or 1,042,560 cubic feet per diem.

In making the estimate of the quantity of water that will be consumed in passing the boats through the locks, let us assume that the canal will enjoy a full trade, and that the boats will pass through the locks at the summit as fast as possible. The average time of a boat passing a lock of 10 feet lift is about six minutes, or 240 per diem. Assuming a full trade we must also assume a fair alternation of boats passing the summit level; if one boat succeed another, each boat will consume two lockfuls of water; if two boats meet on the summit, each boat will consume one lockful of water. It will therefore be fair to assume that the average expenditure of water for boats passing the summit level will be 1½ prisms of lift for each boat, or 360 prisms of lift per diem, which for locks 120 feet long, 20 feet wide and 10 feet lift, would amount to 8,640,000 cubic feet per diem; add to this quantity 1,042,060 cubic feet, the quantity lost by leakage, filtration and evaporation, and we have 9,682,560 cubic feet, or 358,613 cubic yards per diem as the quantity of water necessary to navigate the canal with a full trade.

We have seen that Anthony's creek will afford a nett available supply per day of   571,780 cubic yards,
and that the quantity required for the use of
the canal, will be per day,   358,613 " "
_____
Leaving a surplus for contingencies per day of 213,167 " "

This surplus is amply sufficient to cover any contingencies or objection that ingenuity may suggest, but as a further security there are three other creeks, viz: Little creek, Tuckahoe creek and Howard's creek, whose united volumes amount to about one-third of Anthony's creek, which, if necessary, could be appropriated to the use of the canal.

There ought not then to rest a reasonable doubt in the mind of any candid, sensible man who will take the trouble to investigate this subject, as to the practicability of the passage of the Alleghany by a canal, or as to the sufficiency of the supply of water.

No physical difficulties exist that cannot be overcome by money, for it is not designed to do anything that has not already been done scores of times, both in this country and in Europe.

ESTIMATE OF THE COST OF COMPLETING THE JAMES RIVER AND KANAWHA CANAL FROM BUCHANAN TO THE OHIO RIVER.

In making up this estimate, I have provided for a canal from Buchanan to the Greenbrier river of the same dimensions as the enlarged Erie canal, viz: 42 feet wide at the bottom, 70 feet at the water surface and with a depth of water of 7 feet; the locks to be 120 feet long between the gates, and 20 feet wide; and it is proper to state that the estimate for this portion of the work is based upon a definitive location, and accurate cross sections of the canal for the whole distance.

The estimate for the Greenbrier and New rivers is for steamboat navigation, with stone dams and locks, the locks to be 200 feet long and 40 feet wide, with 7 feet depth of water; extending to Lyken's shoals on the Kanawha where sluice navigation will begin.

ESTIMATE.

1. From Buchanan to Covington	47.27 miles,	$4,036,577
1. From Covington to mouth of Fork run	17.37 "	2,206,795
3. From mouth Fork run to westeren entrance of Alleghany tunnel,	6.03 "	
Including reservoirs and feeders		5,077,736
4. From western end of Alleghany tunnel to Greenbrier river,	9.93 "	1,709,517
5. The Greenbrier river to New river	49.62 "	3,512,506
6. The New river from the mouth of Greenbrier to Lyken's shoals on the Kanawha	73.59 "	9,091,537
7. Kanawha river from Lyken's shoals to the mouth of the Ohio, (sluice improvement)	85.12 "	402,168
Total length of new work,	288.93 miles.	
Total cost from Buchanan to the Ohio river,		$26,036,836

As it would be useless to construct the canal from Buchanan to the Ohio river on an enlarged scale without making a corresponding increase in the size of the locks, and in the depth of the canal from Richmond to Buchanan, I have made an estimate of the cost of building new locks 120 × 20 by the side of the old ones, and of increasing the depth of the water in the canal to 7 feet, which is presented below.

Estimate of the Cost of Doubling the Locks and Deepening the Canal to seven feet, from the Richmond Dock to Buchanan.

New tide-water connection by way of Haxall's mill.....................	334,937
Cost of doubling locks and deepening canal from Richmond to Lynchburg..	2,091,504
Cost of doubling locks and deepening canal from Lynchburg to Buchanan..	1,502,900
Total cost of doubling locks and deepening canal from Richmond dock to Buchanan.......................................	3,929,341
Add cost of new canal from Buchanan to the Ohio river..............	26,036,836
Total cost of completing the Virginia water line.......................	$29,966,177

PROPOSED NEW PLAN FOR SUMMIT LEVEL.

The above estimate is based upon a location of the Summit level, both as to elevation and direction, which was recommended by Capt. McNeil, of U. S. Top. Engineers, in 1827, and has never since been changed. Every route between the headwaters of the James and those of the Greenbrier and New rivers, that gave any promise of being practicable, has been instrumentally examined, and this has proved to have the lowest summit, to be passable at the same elevation with the shortest tunnel, and to afford an abundant supply of water at an inconsiderable expense. There can be no doubt of the superiority of this route over all others; but there may be some question as to the most judicious elevation for the summit level. The choice is between a longer tunnel and less lockage and a shorter tunnel and more lockage. Of course it would be desirable to reduce the lockage as much as possible, both on account of the cost of attendance and the annual repairs of the locks, and the time that would be consumed in passing through them. With that view, after a mature consideration of the subject, I have determined to recommend a change in the plan of passing the summit level, which although more costly, I consider decidedly preferable to the present plan.

I propose to establish the summit at a level 1700 feet above tide, or twenty feet above the level of the Greenbrier river at the mouth of Howard's creek, and pass through the Alleghany mountain by a tunnel about nine miles long. We would thus dispense with 220 feet of lockage on each side of the summit, and with 44 locks; save four miles in distance, and 7½ hours in time, and by feeding directly from the Greenbrier river, be enabled to pass the summit level without the aid of reservoirs.

Let us see whether these advantages will be purchased at too great a cost:

I estimate the cost of a tunnel nine miles long, including a feeder dam on the Greenbrier, at................ 13,790,000

From which, deduct the estimated cost of the alternate route by Howard's and Tuckahoe creeks, including the cost of Anthony's creek reservoir and feeder, 6,392,266

And we find the excess of cost of the short line to be, $7,397,734

To determine whether the company will be justified in expending this large sum of money for the purpose of shortening the distance and the time consumed in lockage, it is necessary first to ascertain the capacity and probable tonnage of the canal and the cost of transportation.

The locks will admit boats about 108 feet long and 19 feet wide, with six feet draft of water: such boats will carry at least 280 tons; but I will put the average loads at 250 tons, and will suppose that one boat will pass through the locks in every 7½ minutes, or 192 boats per day for 300 days, and obtain 14,300,000 tons as the actual capacity of the canal with a full trade. It would be fair then to assume the half of this sum, or say 7,000,000 tons, as the probable tonnage. It will be admitted that for every mile we can shorten the canal, we may expend a capital of which the interest is equal to the annual expense of transporting the whole tonnage over that mile.

By adopting the long tunnel line we save four miles in actual distance, and the time consumed in passing 44 locks, which, at seven and a half minutes to the lock, will amount to 5½ hours, equivalent to a saving of eleven miles more, or a total saving in distance of 15 miles. Assuming the cost of transportation at 4 mills per ton per mile, the passage of 7,000,000 tons over 15 miles will cost $420,000, to which add the annual cost of attendance and repairs of 44 locks at $600 per annum for each lock $26,400, and we have $446,400 for the amount saved annually, which, at six per cent. interest, represents a capital of $7,440,000, which is the amount that may be expended to save a distance of 15 miles. So that if the tonnage should be only one-half of the theoretical capacity of the canal, the company would be justified in incurring the increased expense, in order to have a shorter and better line.*

But some persons may object to so long a tunnel. For my part I cannot see any objections to it, but on the contrary, see everything to recommend it. About its practicability there can be no doubt. The tunnel already excavated through the same mountain for the Covington and Ohio railroad, is about one mile distant from the proposed canal tunnel, is 4,700 feet long, and passes for its entire length through solid slate and sandstone rock. As there have been no extraordinary physical difficulties encountered in excavating this tunnel, none need be apprehended in the canal tunnel, and as will be shown hereafter, it can be completed as speedily as other portions of the work.

I have provided for a tunnel 56 feet wide, and 32 feet high, with a water-way 44 feet wide, and a tow-path of solid mortared masonry on each side six feet wide, so that boats drawn by horses can pass each other without inconvenience; but these tow-paths may be dispensed with, and the tunnel excavated to its full width of 56 feet, may be navigated by steam tugs towing the canal boats through it.

As some intelligent persons and warm advocates of the water-line with whom I have conversed on this subject, have been rather astounded, and have expressed most decided opposition to so long a tunnel, I will here consider the principal objections that have been urged against it.

One is, the stupendous magnitude of the undertaking, and the consequent length of time that will be consumed in its execution. It certainly will be a work of great magnitude, surpassing, both in

---

* NOTE.—The attentive reader will observe a discrepancy in the time allowed for the passage of a boat through the locks in the calculation of the water consumed on the summit level, and in the calculation of the tonnage capacity of the canal, six minutes being assumed in the first case, and seven and a half minutes in the second. This has been done purposely, so as to assume an extravagant average of the quantity of water consumed, and a more moderate and practical average for the assumed capacity of the canal.

its size and length, all others of a similar character in the world. But is that any reason why it should not be done? Ten years ago such an objection would have had some force, and it would have required some temerity to have recommended such a gigantic undertaking. But within that time works of a similar character, and approximating it in magnitude, have been undertaken both in this country and in Europe, and are now being prosecuted to a successful and speedy termination. In this country the Hoosac tunnel in Massachusetts, about four and three-quarter miles long is, in spite of past difficulties and disasters, now progressing favorably. In Europe the Mont Cenis tunnel under the Alps, for the purpose of connecting France and Italy by a continuous railway, is seven and a half miles long, and is now nearly completed. In the interesting report of Mr. Benj'n H. Latrobe, who visited this tunnel last October, there is a statement of the monthly progress of the work, from which it appears that the average monthly progress for the preceding six months from April to October, was 245 feet at one end and 238 feet at the other, or a total of 483 feet per month, or 5,796 feet per annum, more than half a mile a year at each end. The progress of the work on this tunnel, which is being excavated from each end *without the aid of shafts*, and at a monthly *increasing* speed, leads to the most satisfactory assurance that the projected Alleghany tunnel, with the favorable character of the mountain for the location of *numerous shafts*, and the facilities which the late improvements in automatic machine drilling have afforded for the rapid prosecution of that kind of work, could be completed probably as quickly as the rest of the work, certainly as speedily as the 2½ mile tunnel. On the line of the last mentioned tunnel as located, there are three depressions in the mountain at which shafts may be sunk, one 129 feet, one 264 feet, and one 215 feet deep, or three shafts in 2½ miles, averaging 203 feet deep. We may therefore reasonably expect, on the long tunnel line, at least *eight shafts*, or one for each mile of the tunnel, averaging about 425 feet deep. But if there is only one shaft for every three miles of the tunnel, and one year is allowed for sinking them, it is evident that at the rate of half a mile a year each way from each shaft, and from the ends, the tunnel could be excavated in four years from its commencement, which is about as quickly as the New river or Greenbrier sections could be completed under the most favorable circumstances. No reasonable objection, then, can be urged against the long tunnel on account of the time that will be consumed in its execution. It is simply a question of money and of money only, and I think that I have proved that the money would be economically and judiciously expended.

Another objection is urged as to its use after it is completed, a fancied difficulty and even horror of passing for a distance of nine miles underground and in utter darkness. It will be observed that I have provided for towpaths of masonry six feet wide on each side of the tunnel, which are to be protected on their edges by a cast iron curb or railing. By this means there will be ample room and perfect security for teams, and as there will be no meeting of teams nor passing of lines under or over the boats, there will be no delay when the boats pass each other as there is elsewhere, and consequently the navigation through the tunnel will be conducted with less delay and inconvenience, and with as much security as on other parts of the line.

As to the darkness, the boats, of course, will have their bow lights up, which will give a sufficiency of light. I believe that if the boatmen had the choice of the two routes, they would greatly prefer the nine miles through the long tunnel to the fourteen miles by the other route, with its 440 feet of lockage and its two and a half miles tunnel, and its delay of 7½ hours. In fact there is no objection that is urged against the nine mile tunnel, except as to its cost, that cannot be applied to a tunnel 2½ miles long, and the summit cannot be passed by a tunnel of less length. To get up to this level there is an ascent from the Greenbrier river of 240 feet and a corresponding descent on the other side, occupying in all a distance of 14 miles. To feed the canal by this route and at this level we have to resort to a reservoir on Anthony's creek, a feeder canal nine miles long, and a feeder tunnel 2½ miles long. By the alternate route we have a tunnel nearly four times as long, but equally as practicable in its construction and use; we shorten the distance actually four miles, and in effect fifteen, dispense with 44 locks and the expense of their attendance and maintenance, and by feeding directly from the Greenbrier river, avoid the necessity of resorting to a reservoir and feeder canal to supply the summit level with water.

Moreover, by avoiding the delay attending the passing of so many locks so close together we would actually increase the capacity and value of the canal, and would present to the consideration of the public an improvement which when completed will in its capacity and utility, be superior to any other on this continent.

Anticipating that there might be criticisms adverse to the proposed change of plan at the summit level, I have not been contented to recommend such an extensive tunnel solely upon my own judgment, but have solicited the advice of a gentleman whose opinion upon such a subject, is probably entitled to more respect and confidence than that of any other engineer in this country. I allude to Mr. Benjamin H. Latrobe, of Baltimore, whose long experience in tunnelling, and especially as consulting engineer of the Hoosac tunnel, and whose observation of the operations at the Mont Cenis tunnel have afforded him rare opportunities of acquiring an enlightened judgment concerning the practicability, and the probable time that would be consumed in the prosecution of a work of such magnitude as the proposed Alleghany tunnel. I have the pleasure of presenting his letter on that subject, which he has kindly permitted to be published.

BALTIMORE, May 1st, 1868.

E. LORRAINE, Esq.,
Engineer and Superintendent James River
and Kanawha Canal, Richmond, Va.

DEAR SIR:—I am in receipt of your letter of the 30th ultimo, and of the map and report accompanying it, and which contains the most specific information you are able to give me as to the profile of the proposed long tunnel at the summit level of the James River and Kanawha Canal. I would, of course, have liked to have had before me an accurate longitudinal section of the line of the tunnel, but the heights above tide shown upon the topographical map, and the projection of the position of the work thereon, enable me to say what follows in the way of an opinion, which, if it will assist you in recommending the enterprise, I shall feel glad to have given, desiring as I do, the success of every effort to improve the communications of our common country, aside from all local interests.

I cannot hesitate to pronounce the proposed tunnel of 10 miles in length *entirely practicable*, nor do I doubt that, for the reasons assigned in your letter to me, it would be expedient to adopt it instead of the shorter one of 2 6-10 miles. The assumed summit level of the canal being 1700 feet above tide, and the highest surface elevation at the top of the Alleghany mountain over the tunnel being but 2606 feet above tide, if one or more shafts had to be sunk even at points as high as this, they would still be not excessive in depth. I judge, however, from an inspection of the map, that if the line of the tunnel be curved as you suggest, and to which I see no serious objection (the radii being large), the extreme depth of shaft need not exceed 600 or 700 feet, and the average depth about 400 feet. If then, we assume a shaft in each mile, we can estimate the time required to execute the work with some certainty. Experience in sinking the deep central shaft of the Hoosac tunnel of 1030 feet in depth, has shown that in the mica slate rock of that mountain, a speed of 25 feet per month can be made in drilling by hand labor and blasting with common gunpowder. In the clay slates and sandstones of the Alleghany mountain, I believe that a progress of from 30 to 40 feet per month could be effected, even by hand-drilling, and considerably more by machine drills and nitro-glycerine. If we assume then but 33⅓ feet per month, the shafts of 400 feet average depth can be sunk in twelve months after being fairly started, and as they may be simultaneously begun and finished, the work of drifting horizontally in the body of the tunnel could be commenced at two faces in each shaft, or twenty faces in the whole ten shafts, supposing the whole tunnel to be taken out through the shafts, and allowing nothing for the approach cuts. There would then be half a mile to drive each way from each shaft; and at an average rate of but 100 feet per month, the several workings would meet in 26 4-10 months, or a little over two years. Adding to this the twelve months employed in sinking the shafts, we have 3 years and 2 4-10 months, and with a further addition of enough time for preparation and contingencies to make up four years, the work could be finished and in operation at the end of that period. It may seem incredible that a ten mile tunnel could be finished in any such time, and if the time already spent at the Hoosac and at Mont Cenis, be taken as settling the question, it would be at once decided adversely to this estimate. But we must look at the *recent* progress of those works, with the advantage of the experience earned by them and now available to a new scheme of similar character, and not to the *average* progress, including the delays attendant upon mistakes made in the outset, and the defects of the labor-saving machinery which has since been perfected and is now realizing such vastly improved results.

Having driven more than one tunnel in slates and sandstones, such as will be met with in the Alleghany tunnel you have projected, I am well acquainted with the character of those rocks, and know that very rapid progress can be made in them. The strike and dip of the strata at your locality are also as favorable as possible to safe and speedy working. I assume that the most improved drilling machine will be used, and that, as suggested in my last report upon the Hoosac tunnel, which you have, the whole section be taken out at once, without any preliminary "heading," which can be readily done with drill carriages properly constructed for the purpose. I also suppose that nitro-glycerine would be used as the explosive, although that would not be necessary to insure a progress of 100 feet per month, much more than which has been effected with gunpowder, both at Mont Cenis (where as much as 272 feet per month has been accomplished) and at the Hoosac, where 131 feet has been driven in a much harder and tougher rock than either that of Mont Cenis or the Alleghany mountain.

As much water may be encountered in your long tunnel, the most effective means of raising it must be provided, and for this purpose no engine can be compared with the Cornish engine (of the "bull" form) placed at the *top of the shaft*. The hoisting and ventilating machinery must of course be of the most approved form, and in short all the operations within and without the tunnel made to harmonize in the most perfect manner.

In conclusion I will add that I have never felt, in giving a professional opinion, more perfect confidence in its soundness, and the certainty with which the results predicted can be realized.

I am, dear sir, yours respectfully and truly,

BENJ. H. LATROBE,
. *Civil Engineer.*

The estimated cost of the improvement by the long line is	$29,966,177
Add excess of cost of short line,	7,397,734
Total cost by short line,	$37,363,911

The value of the Improvement as an Investment.

Capital invested in new works, say	$40,000,000
" " old " "	4,926,664
Preferred six per cent. stock of the state	7,400,000
Total capital invested,	$52,326,664

Assumed Revenue.

7,000,000 tons through freight, 485 miles @ 2 mills per ton per mile,	$6,790,000
100,000 " way " say 50 " @ 1 cent per ton per mile,	50,000
200,000 " to and from Lynchburg, 146 miles @ ¾ cent per ton per mile,	219,000
100,000 " to and from Buchanan and Lexington, 196 miles @ ½ cent per ton per mile	98,000
200,000 tons to and from Covington, 243 miles @ 4 mills per ton per mile,	194,400
300,000 ⁻ coal from Kanawha valley to Lynchburg, and to Iron furnaces on line of canal, 250 miles, @ 2.5 mills per ton per mile	187,500
200,000 tons coal from Kanawha valley to Richmond, 400 miles @ 2 mills per ton per mile	160,000
500,000 tons coal from Kanawha valley to New York and other eastern cities, via Richmond, 400 miles at 2 mills per ton per mile	400,000
Revenue from tonnage of Kanawha westward	400,000
Revenue from Richmond dock	400,000

Revenue from water rents..	30,000
Revenue from boats and passengers....................................	100,000
	$9,028,900
Expenses of repairs and administration $750 per mile,	303,750
Nett revenue,	$8,665,150
Which is more than 16 per cent. on a capital of	$53,000,000

The coal field penetrated by the Kanawha, Coal, Big Sandy and Guyandotte rivers, in the variety, quality and quantity of its Bituminous coals, is without parallel on this continent. The Virginia water-line opens this entire field to eastern markets. The Kanawha passes through the heart of this coal region, and the Coal river, its tributary, is already provided with slack-water navigation. The cannel coal of this coal basin can certainly be delivered in New York city by the Virginia water-line at one-half of the present cost in that city by the cargo of the English cannel coal. It is difficult to estimate the advantages of the Virginia water-line to the east in connection with this coal, but great confidence is felt that the above estimate of eastern shipments will, on the completion of the water-line, be found to be far below the mark.

VALUE OF THE IMPROVEMENT TO THE WESTERN AND NORTHWESTERN STATES.

But it is not only as a profitable investment for capital, but chiefly in its character as a great public highway, by which the products of agriculture, the forest and mines may find 'the shortest and cheapest means of access to the eastern markets, that this great improvement recommends itself especially to the consideration of the people of the western and northwestern states.

These states are almost exclusively agricultural, and produce an immense surplus of grain and pork, which is increasing every year to an extent that is incalculable. The states of Missouri, Illinois, Iowa, Wisconsin and Minnesota are estimated to have produced more than one-fourth of the whole value of the crops raised in the United States in 1864, four-tenths of all the wheat, and nearly one-half of all the corn. Nearly all the wheat exported from this country is sent from those states.

New England produces but eleven quarts of wheat to each inhabitant, and consumes $50,000,000 more than she produces of agricultural productions. Even Pennsylvania and New York are calling upon the teeming granaries of the west to supply their deficiency in breadstuffs, and Ohio is barely making a surplus.* England imports 72 million bushels of wheat annually, and her importations are increasing every year, and in Europe generally the deficiency of grain must be greater every year, for the production is nearly at a stand while the population is steadily increasing. This rapidly multiplying deficiency of breadstuffs in the old world and in the east can be supplied only from the western and northwestern states, which will soon become the granary of the world.

The great question, then, with the people of those states, is how to get their surplus productions to market in the shortest time and at the least possible cost, for their success and wealth depend very much on the cost of transportation. The prices of wheat, corn and pork in the west are regulated by the prices of those articles in New York, being generally the same, less the cost of transportation to that place.

The surplus products of the west are estimated at 25 million tons. The chief channels of communication with the east, are by the Mississippi river to New Orleans, and thence by gulf and ocean to New York or Liverpool, and by a variety of railroads, crossing the northwestern states east of the Mississippi to the lake cities, and then either by the lakes and Erie canal or by direct railroad line to New York.

These railroads charge enormous freights, but possess a great advantage in the element of time. They deliver freight from the Mississippi river into New York in about ten days, and the merchant in the western city is thus enabled to draw at ten days' sight on his New York commission merchant and get his draft discounted at bank, and invest his money in new purchases. The facilities thus offered by these routes enable them at extortionate prices to compete to their utmost capacity with the river route, with its low rates but long time.

"The directors of the bureau of statistics have completed an elaborate report for one of the committees of congress, which shows the tonnage and value of the freight transported during the year ended March 31st, 1867, across the state of Illinois, westward of the meridian of Chicago, from which it appears that there was

---

*See speech of P. Robb, Esq., before the Mississippi river improvement convention held at Dubuque, Iowa, Feb. 15th, 1866.

transported over eight railroads running eastward, 4,358,000 tons of freight, the value of which amounted to $235,000,000; and westward 1,345,000 tons valued at $411,000,000. The combined movement amounting to the enormous aggregate of 5,703,000 tons valued at $646,000,000, an amount nearly equal to two-thirds of the entire freight commerce of the country." We thus find that these railroads only transport about one-sixth part of the estimated surplus products of the west.

In a letter written by Mr. Thomas M. Monroe, and published in the Dubuque Times, January 28th, 1868, he says: "The charges by railroad from Dubuque (188 miles west of Chicago) and New York are now for the lowest class freight carried eastward, one dollar and ten cents per hundred, or twenty-two dollars per ton.

In the summer when canal and lake navigation was free, it was ninety-five cents per hundred or nineteen dollars per ton. The lowest rate on westward bound freight is now one dollar and thirty cents per hundred or twenty-six dollars per ton, while the next class of heavy freight pays two dollars and thirty cents per hundred or forty-six dollars per ton. This is nearly as favorable a point from which to transport produce or merchandise from the Mississippi across to New York, or *vice versa*, as any other point west of that stream, as it is nearly in the line of the general route of transportation. It may therefore be safely stated that transportations on produce paying the lowest charges from any point on the western bank of the Mississippi to New York will not fall short of an average throughout the year of $20 per ton; and the westward bound freight is still higher."

In the Dubuque Herald of March 18th, 1868, it is stated that the Mississippi Barge Company have advertised the following rates for the coming season:

Wheat from St. Paul to New York		36 cts. per bushel.
Do " Dubuque " "		32 " "
Corn " Illinois river to "		28 " "

These rates are on an average cheaper than shipments from Chicago to New York via the lakes in the summer time.

"The Des Moines Iowa Register of the 15th March, 1868, says: The first shipment since the war from Liverpool by New Orleans, the Mississippi river and the Des Moines Valley railroad to Des Moines was made a few days ago; 27 crates of queensware came through in 95 days, at the cost of 84 cents per hundred pounds less than via the Atlantic cities, and at a cost of only $1 17 per hundred pounds from Liverpool. We are also of the opinion that this is cheaper than the regular carrying price from Liverpool to Chicago."

As an illustration of the value of the Virginia water-line to the people of the northwestern states, let us now make a comparison of the cost of transporting a bushel of wheat from Dubuque to New York via river and ocean, and the cost of transporting it by the Virginia water-line to the seaboard.

Wheat from Dubuque to New York, 1665 miles by river, and 1850 miles by ocean, total 3,515 miles at 32 cents per bushel=$10 56 per ton, or 3 mills per ton per mile. Distributing the charges in proper proportion would give for the ocean transportation $2\frac{1}{10}$ mills per ton per mile, and for the river transportation 4 mills per ton per mile.

The cost of transportation on the Erie canal is stated at 4 mills per ton per mile, exclusive of tolls. As will be shown hereafter, transportation on the Virginia canal will be equally as cheap as on the Erie. I therefore put it at 4 mills, and adding 2 mills for tolls, make the whole charges on the James River and Kanawha Canal 6 mills per ton per mile.

The charges then on wheat from Dubuque to Hampton roads by the Virginia water-line will be as follows:

River transportation from Dubuque to Point Pleasant, 1,367 miles, at 4 mills per
ton per mile.. $5 47
Point Pleasant to Richmond, 485 miles, @ 6 mills.. 2 91
Richmond to Hampton roads, 125 miles, @ 4 mills... 50
One transshipment... 10

$8 98

Difference in favor of Virginia line 1.58 cents per ton, or nearly five cents per bushel.

It will thus be seen that the Virginia water-line can compete successfully with the Mississippi river and ocean line from the northwestern states even at the low prices advertised by the Mississippi Barge Company; and when we take into consideration the great saving in time and insurance by the Virginia line, the liability of breadstuffs to heat and sour by passing through a damp semitropical climate, who can doubt that the great bulk of the surplus products of the northwestern states will seek a market through Virginia.

We have seen that the lowest rates charged by the comparatively short railroad routes from Dubuque to New York in the summer, when canal and lake navigation was open, was nineteen dollars a ton. There would be a saving then of $10 02 per ton in transportation by the Virginia water-line to the seaboard over the railroad line from Dubuque to New York, or about $40,000,000 a year on the eastward bound freight only, enough in one year to pay the whole estimated cost of constructing the canal on the most expensive scale.

I have compared the cost of transportation from Dubuque to New York with that from the same place to Hampton roads, because the completion of the canal will demand, and be sure to result in, the establishment of a port of entry at Hampton roads or the mouth of James river, which must in a short time grow to be a large city, with regular commercial relations established between it and Europe. This future great commercial emporium of Virginia will, through its connection by the Virginia water-line with the western states, and because nearer and more accessible by railroad to at least seven-eighths of the Mississippi valley than any Atlantic city north of it, be the point of transhipment of their immense freights to be conveyed by ocean steamers and sailing vessels to all parts of the world. It will be connected by a continuous water line, 1,880 miles long with Kansas city, and one 2,224 miles long, with Omaha on the Missouri river, which are the termini of the Union Pacific railroad, now in the course of completion to San Francisco. The immense trade that will pour into these cities from both directions will, of course, bring with it a corresponding travel, and Virginia will become the great thoroughfare both for trade and travel between Europe and California and the other Pacific States. All that Commodore Matthew F. Maury said of Norfolk may be said of this future port of Virginia: "*As to natural advantages of position, depth of water and accessibility by land and sea, Norfolk has no competitor among the seaport towns of the Atlantic.* Midway the Atlantic coast line of the United States, Norfolk is the most convenient because the most central point where the produce of the interior may be collected; and whence it may be distributed, north and south, right and left, among the markets of the seaboard. Its climate is delightful; it is exactly of that happy middle temperature where the frosts of the north bite not, and where the pestilence of the south walketh not. Its harbor is commodious, and as safe as can be. It is never blocked up with ice, and as to the egress and ingress between it and the sea, it possesses all the facilities that the mariner could desire.

"Moreover, the prevailing winds in the parallel of Norfolk are westerly winds, which are fair for coasting and for going seaward in any direction. A little to the south of that parallel you find the northeast trades, which are fair winds for the inward bound Norfolk vessels.

"Then there is the gulf stream, that mighty river in the ocean, upon the verge of which Norfolk stands.

"It flows up with a current which, without the help of sweeps, sails or steam, will carry the European bound vessels out of Norfolk at the rate of nearly one hundred miles a day, directly on her course. Then at the sides of this, and counter to it, are eddies which favor the same vessel on her return to Norfolk. · These *hawse* her along and shorten her voyage by many a mile.

"Such are the natural advantages of Norfolk seaward. Let us look ashore and consider them landward, and compare them with the natural inland advantages of New York. Stretch a string on the map from Norfolk to New York and make a dot half way between them. Now seek a point on the south shore of lake Erie that is equidistant from New York and Norfolk; draw a line from the dot to this point, and you will have a dividing line of distance between the two places, every point along which will be just as far from the one place as the other. You will find that this line runs through Delaware and cuts lake Erie near Cleveland, Ohio.

"Thus you perceive that Chicago, in Illinois, and St. Louis, Missouri, are actually nearer to Norfolk than they are to New York, even by an air line.

"You see, moreover, that as between New York and Norfolk, the natural advantages here are greatly in favor of the latter.

" *The most direct way to the sea through either of these ports, from most of the lake country, and from almost the entire Mississippi valley, lies through Virginia.* The natural advantages, then, of Norfolk in relation to the sea, or to the back country, are superior beyond comparison to those of New York."

Whether, then, the future seaport of Virginia be Norfolk or a new city to be built on the north side of the mouth of James river, we have the highest authority in this country or in any other, for pronouncing it *the most capacious, safe, accessible* and *convenient* harbor from Florida to New Foundland.

Its depth of water is sufficient to float the Great Eastern, and its capacity to accommodate the shipping of the world.

It is proper, therefore, in making a comparison of distances and charges, to make Hampton roads, the Atlantic terminus of the Virginia water-line, the point of comparison with New York.

COMPARATIVE COST OF TRANSPORTATION, BY THE VIRGINIA WATER LINE AND OTHER COMPETING ROUTES, FROM THE PRINCIPAL WESTERN CITIES TO THE ATLANTIC SEABOARD.

The previous comparisons were made upon the actually existing *charges* for transportation between New York and Dubuque (this city being selected because it is a point of comparison as favorable to the northern lines of transportation as any other on the upper Mississippi, and about midway between St. Louis and St. Paul), but inasmuch as the charges for transportation are fluctuating, and dependent a good deal upon the competition produced by rival lines, it will be proper to make the comparison between the Virginia water-line and other routes upon the more certain fixed basis of the actual cost of transportation.

The costs of transportation as laid down by Mr. W. J. McAlpine, state engineer and surveyor of the New York canals in 1854, and which he stated had been arrived at with great care, were as follows:

Ocean—Transportation, average............................1.5 mills.
Lakes—Long...2.0 mills.
    Short...3.4 mills.
Rivers—Hudson and of similar character....................2.5 mills.
    Mississippi and Ohio......................................3.0 mills.
Canal—Erie enlargement......................................4.0 mills.
    Ordinary size..5.0 mills.
Railroads—Average..15.0 mills.

The cost of transportation may be somewhat greater now than it was then, in consequence of the general advance in the prices of labor, provisions and materials; but as any changes of that kind will apply equally to all kinds of transportation, the relative cost will still remain the same, and therefore the above figures will subserve the purpose of comparison just as well now as then, and may be relied upon as being very nearly correct.

The locks on the enlarged Erie canal are 110 feet long in the chamber, and 18 feet wide. The largest boats are 98 feet long, 17.4 feet wide, and draw 6.4 feet water, their maximum capacity being 240 tons.

6

As the locks on the James River and Kanawha canal, as proposed, will be 120 feet long and 20 feet wide in the chamber, they will admit boats of larger dimensions and greater capacity than those on the Erie canal. I estimate their capacity at 280 tons. The lockage on the J. R. and K. canal will be much greater than on the Erie, but taking in consideration the greater capacity of the · canal and the fact that it will have at its western end 85 miles of open river navigation and 123 miles of slackwater, adapted to steamboats, we certainly will be justifiable in assuming the cost of transportation on the Virginia water-line from Point Pleasant to Richmond at 4 mills per ton per mile.

The following tables show the comparative cost of transportation by the leading routes from the west and northwest to the Atlantic ports.

The inland distances are taken from Williams' and Appleton's Traveller's Guide Books, and the ocean distances have been kindly furnished from the coast survey office at Washington.

No. 1.

From Dubuque, Iowa, to Hampton Roads, by the Virginia Water-line.

Dubuque to Point Pleasant,	1,367 miles @ 3 mills per ton per mile			$4 10
Pt. Pleasant to Richmond,	485 "	4 "	" "	1 94
Richmond to Hampton roads,	125 "	3 "	" "	38

1,977

One transhipment.. 10

$6 52

No. 2.

From Dubuque, Iowa, to New York, by Railroad.

Dubuque to Chicago by Galena and Chicago R. R. 188 miles.
Chicago to Dunkirk by Lake Shore R. R............. 497 "
Dunkirk to New York by Erie R. R.................... 460 "

Dubuque to New York, 1145 " @ 15.0 mills $17 17
Difference in favor of Virginia route $10 65 per ton.
" against " in distance, 832. miles.

No. 3.

Dubuque to New York, via Chicago, the Lakes and Erie Canal.

Dubuque to Chicago by railroad...........	188 miles	@	15.0	mills	✕ 10	2	92
Chicago to Buffalo by the lakes............	1042 "	"	2	"	✕ 10	2	18
Buffalo to West Troy by Erie Canal......	350 "	"	4	"		1	40
West Troy to New York by Hudson river	151 "	"	2.5	"			38

1731 "	$6 88

Difference in favor of the Virginia line, 36 cts. per ton.
"   against   "   in distance, 246 miles.

No. 4.

Dubuque to New York, via Toledo and the Lake and Erie Canal.

Dubuque to Toledo by railroad...........	432 miles	@	15.0	mills	✕ 10	$6	58
Toledo to Buffalo by lake..................	252 "	"	3	"	✕ 10		86
Buffalo to New York, as by No. 3.......	501 "	"				1	78

1185	$9 22

Difference in favor of Virginia line 2 70 per ton.
"   against   "   in distance, 792 miles.

No. 5.

From Dubuque to New York, via Mississippi river and Ocean.

Dubuque to New Orleans, 1,665 miles @ 3 mills..............................	4	99
New Orleans to New York 1,850 " 1½ mills ✕ 10 cents................	2	87

3,515	$7 86

Difference in favor of Virginia line $1 34 cents
"   "   "   "   "   1,538 miles.

No. 6.

From St. Louis to Hampton Roads, by Virginia Water-line.

St. Louis to Point Pleasant 903 miles @ 3 mills ✕ 10.......................	$2	81
Pt. Pleasant to Richmond 485 " 4 "	1	94
Richmond to Hampton rds. 125 " 3 "		38

1,513	$5 13

No. 7.

From St. Louis to New York, via Illinois and Michigan Canal, Lakes and Erie Canal.

St. Louis to Grafton	41 miles @ 3 mills....................	0 12
Grafton to Peru, Illinois river	274 " 4 mills ⋈ 10...........	1 20
Peru to Chicago by canal	102 " 5 " ⋈ 10...........	61
Chicago to New York via the lakes	1,543 by table No. 3....................	3 96
	1,960	$5 89

Difference in favor of Virginia line 76 cents per ton.
"   "   "   "   447 miles.

No. 8.

St. Louis to New York, via Portsmouth, Ohio and Erie Canals.

St. Louis to Portsmouth, Ohio river,	811 miles, @ 3 mills, ⋈ 10,	2 53
Portsmouth to Cleaveland by canal,	307 miles, @ 5 mills, ⋈ 10,	1 63
Cleaveland to Buffalo by lake,	194 miles, @ 3.4 "	66
Buffalo to New York by Erie canal,	501 table No. 3,	1 88
	1813	$6 70

Difference in favor of Virginia, $1 57 per ton.
Do   do   do,   300 miles.

From St. Louis and Cairo to New York by Mississippi river and ocean, the difference in favor of the Virginia route will be the same as from Dubuque, and 223 miles below Cairo or about Memphis, Tennessee, the cost by the two routes will be equal.

For Cairo, Louisville, Cincinnati and all other points on the Ohio river between Cairo and Portsmouth, via the Ohio and Erie Canals to New York, the difference in favor of the Virginia route will be the same as for St. Louis, in table No. 8, but of course the proportional saving will be greater, because it will be the same amount saved on a smaller total of costs.

No. 9.

Evansville to New York, by Wabash Canal, Lakes and Erie Canal.

Evansville to Toledo,	467 miles, @ 5 mills, ⋈ 10....................	2 43
Toledo to New York,	753 miles, by No. 4....................	2 64
	1220	$5 07

Evansville to Hampton Roads by Virginia Water-Line.

Evansville to Point Pleasant,   530 miles, @ 3 mills, ⋈ 10......... 1 69
Point Pleasant to Hampton Roads,   610 by No. 6........................... 2 32

                          1140 $4 01
Difference in favor of Virginia water-line, $1 06 cents.
Do   do   do   in distance, 80 miles.

No. 10.

Cincinnati to New York, by Miami Canal, Lake and Erie Canal.

Cincinnati to Toledo, 266 miles, @ 5 mills, ⋈ 10............................ 1 43
Toledo to New York, 753 miles, by No. 4,   2 64

                    1019 $4 07

Cincinnati to Hampton Roads, by Virginia Water-Line.

Cincinnati to Point Pleasant,   206 miles, @ 3 mills, ⋈ 10...........   72
Point Pleasant to Hampton Roads, 610 miles, by No. 6....................... 2 32

                    816              $3 04
Difference in favor of Virginia water-line, $1 03 cents.
Do   do   do   in distance, 203 miles.

No. 11.

Wheeling to Baltimore, via Baltimore and Ohio Railroad.

Three hundred and eighty miles @ 15.0 mills per ton per mile...............$5 70

Wheeling to Hampton Roads by Virginia Water-Line.

Wheeling to Point Pleasant   177 miles, @ 3 mills, ⋈ 10.............   63
Pt. Pleasant to Hampton Roads, 610 miles, by table No. 6................. 2 32

                    787              $2 95
Difference in favor of Virginia line, $2 75.
Do against in distance, 407 miles.

No. 12.

St. Louis to Liverpool, via New Orleans.

St. Louis to New Orleans, 1201 miles, @ 3 mills, ⋈ 10......'............... 3 70
N. Orleans to Liverpool, 5328 miles, @ 1½ mills.............................. 7 99

                  6529 $11 69

St. Louis to Liverpool, via Virginia Water-Line.

St Louis to Hampton Roads,	1513 miles, by table No. 6..............	5 13
Hampton Roads to Liverpool,	3710 miles, @ 1½ mills, ⋈ 10..........	5 66
	5223	$10 79

Difference in favor of the Virginia route, 90 cents.
Difference in favor of, in distance, 1306 miles.

Besides the cost of transportation in the above table being in favor of the Virginia route, the difference in time, in climate, in safety, in insurance, and in preservation of the cargo, will also be so much in favor of that route, that there can be but little doubt it will be the one selected for direct exports and imports between St. Louis and Liverpool; and as St. Louis is destined to be the great central city of the west to which will converge the mighty trade of the yet undeveloped far west, which will be brought in by the several railroads that are now stretching out their arms toward the Pacific, it appears that St. Louis, more than any other city of the west, should feel a lively and peculiar interest in the completion of the Virginia water-line.

The crates of queensware, noticed above, that were imported from Liverpool to Des Moines, Iowa, in 95 days, at $1 17 per hundred, might have been imported by the Virginia water-line in 45 days at a cost of $1 00 per hundred.

No. 13.

Cincinnati to Liverpool, via New Orleans.

Cincinnati to New Orleans..............	1548 miles @ 3 mills ⋈ 10 cts.	4 74
New Orleans to Liverpool..............	5328 " " 1½ "	7 99
	6876 "	$12 73

Cincinnati to Liverpool, via Virginia Water-Line.

Cincinnati to Pt. Pleasant.....................	206 miles @ 3 mills ⋈ 10 cts.	72
Pt. Pleasant to Hampton Roads........... .	610 " by table No. 6.........	2 32
Hampton Roads to Liverpool..............	3710 " @ 1½ mills ⋈ 10 cts.	5 66
	4526	$8 70

Difference in favor of Virginia water-line $4 03.
   do.   do.   do.   in distance 2350 miles.

As it has already been shown that the difference between Cincinnati and New York, and Cincinnati and Hampton Roads, was $1 03 cts. per ton in favor of the latter route, and as importations could be made as cheaply from Liverpool to Hampton Roads as to New York, it will be decidedly to the interest of Cincinnati to make her European exports and imports by the Virginia route in preference to any other, both in view of time and expense; and the same may be said of Louisville, Kentucky.

No. 14.

Memphis, Tenn., to Norfolk by railroad, 956 miles @ 15 mills................... $14 34

Memphis, Tenn., to Hampton Roads, by Virginia Water-Line.

Memphis to Pt. Pleasant.................. 973 miles @ 3 mills ⋈ 10........... 3 02
Pt. Pleasant to Hampton Roads........ 610   "   table No. 6................... 2 32
—
1583 $5 34

Difference in favor of Virginia water-line $9 per ton.
  do.   against   do.   in distance 627 miles.

GENERAL SUMMARY.

ROUTES.	Distance.	Cost per ton.	Distance in favor of water-line.	Distance against water-line.	Cost in favor of water line.
		$ c.			$ c.
Dubuque to Hampton roads by Virginia water-line......	1,977	6 52	......		
Do. to New York by railroads..................	1,145	17 17	......	832	10 65
Do. to New York by Chicago, lakes and Erie canal,	1,731	6 88	....	246	36
Do. to do. by Toledo, do. do. do. do.,	1,185	9 22	....	792	2 70
Do. to do. by Mississippi and ocean...........	3,515	7 86	1,538		1 34
St. Louis to Hampton roads by Virginia water-line......	1,513	5 13	......		
Do. to New York by Illinois and Michigan and Erie canals...................................	1,960	5 89	447		76.
St. Louis to New York by Portsmouth, Ohio and Erie canals..	1,813	6 70	300		1 57
St. Louis to New York by Mississippi river and ocean,	3,051	6 47	......		1 34
Louisville to Hampton roads by Virginia water-line.....	9·19	3 44	......		
Do. to New York by Portsmouth, Ohio and Erie canals......................................	1,249	5 01	300		1 57
Evansville to Hampton roads by Virginia water-line...	1,140	4 01	......		
Do. to New York by Wabash and Erie canals....	1,220	5 07	80		1 06
Cincinnati to Hampton roads by Virginia water-line....	816	3 04	......		
Do. to New York by Portsmouth, Ohio and Erie canals......................................	1,116	4 61	300		1 57
Cincinnati to New York by Miami and Erie canals......	1,019	4 07	203		1 03
Do. to New York by Mississippi river and ocean,	3,398	7 51	2,582		4 47
Wheeling to Baltimore by Baltimore and Ohio railroad,	380	5 70	......		
Do. to Hampton roads by Virginia water-line.....	787	2 95	......	407	2 75
St. Louis to Liverpool by New Orleans......................	6,529	11 69	......		
Do. to do. by Virginia water-line..............	5,223	10 79	1,306		90
Cincinnati to Liverpool by New Orleans..................	6,876	12 73	......		
Do. to Liverpool by Virginia water-line............	4,526	8 70	2,350		4 03
Louisville to Liverpool by New Orleans....................	6,743	12 33	......		
Louisville to Liverpool by Virginia water-line...........:	4.659	9 10	1,863		3 23
Memphis to Norfolk by railroad..................	956	14 34	......		
Do. to do. by Virginia water-line.................	1,583	5 34	......	627	9 00

It appears from the above tables that the country bordering on the Ohio river from Wheeling to its mouth, and on the eastern side of the Mississippi from the mouth of the Ohio up to St. Paul, and all the country west of the Mississippi river between these points, including a large part of Ohio, Indiana, Illinois, Wisconsin and Kentucky, the whole of Missouri, Iowa, Minnesota, Kansas, Nebraska and Dakota, will be tributary to the Virginia water-line, and may find through Virginia, in most cases the shortest, and in all cases the cheapest route to the Atlantic seaboard.

CLIMATIC ADVANTAGE OF THE VIRGINIA WATER-LINE.

The Virginia route has another very decided advantage over the northern water-lines, in its being located in a more temperate climate, in consequence of which it will be open at least four months in the year when the northern canals will be closed by ice.

By examining the reports of the James River and Kanawha Company it will be seen that from 1840 to 1848, there was no suspension of navigation by ice reported, except twelve days in 1845. If there were any others they must have been so slight as not to have attracted attention, or to have been deemed unworthy of comment. From 1848 to the present time, all suspensions of navigation by ice have been reported by the superintendents and have been as follows:

Years.	Days of suspension.
1848-49	8 days.
1849-50	none.
1850-51	none.
1851-52	32 days.
1852-53	none.
1853-54	none.
1854-55	23 days.
1855-56	55 days.
1856-57	56 days.
1857-58	none.
1858-59	none.
1859-60	16 days.
1860-61	none.
1861-62	none.
1862-63	none.
1863-64	21 days.
1864-65	none.
1865-66	8 days.
1866-67	42 days.
1867-68	41 days.

We find then that in a period of twenty years the total number of days in which the navigation was suspended by ice, amounts to 302, an average of 15 days for each year. As these reports apply to the canal as high up as Buchanan, west of the Blue Ridge, it will be reasonable to infer that when the canal reaches its highest elevation in the Alleghanies, it will not be closed by ice on an average more than thirty days in the year, while the Erie canal is closed by ice about five months in the year, making a difference of one-third of the year in favor of the Virginia water-line, and that at the very season of the year when the agricultural products of the west are seeking an eastern market.

CANALS NOT BEHIND THE AGE.

There has been an opinion prevailing for many years in Virginia that the days of canals are numbered, and that they must be superseded by railroads. The only reason that I have ever heard for this condemnation of canals is, that they are "too slow" and "behind the spirit of the age." But this is mere empty assertion without any argument in support of it. The real question is, which can transport the products of agriculture, of the forest and mines, at the least cost, railroads or canals; and as the spirit of the age is decidedly money-making, it would seem that the improvement by which the most money can be made or saved, would be the very one that was not behind the spirit of the age. It will not be controverted that a canal can transport more tonnage and at less cost than a railroad. Instances, no doubt, may be produced where railroads have carried freight at as low or even lower price than canals; but if they have done so, it has always been at a loss, and under peculiar circumstances produced by the irregularities of trade, and by competition with canals.

Thus canals not only transport cheaply themselves, but they are the cause of cheap transportation on railroads, and are thereby a double blessing to the state. Take away from the railroads the wholesome competition of water carriage, and the community immediately suffers from their rapacity, as may be witnessed every winter on the lake shore roads as soon as the navigation is closed by ice.

In proof of the assertion, that canals can transport more tonnage and at less cost than railroads, take the following statement of the comparative business of the New York canals and railroads for the year 1866, which is the latest report that has been printed:

The total number of tons carried on all the railroads of the state during the year, from the 1st October, 1865, to 30th September, 1866, was 9,210,476, and on the canals, during the season of navigation, which was 226 days, 5,775,220, the canals transporting more per month than the railroads.

The following table, taken from the report of the auditor of the New York state canals, shows the total movement of tons on the two railways connecting New York with Lake Erie, and on the state canals, during the year 1866, the freight paid to the roads, and the tolls and carrier's charges on the canals:

1866.	Total Tonnage.	Tons moved one mile.	Freight and Tolls.	Average per ton per mile.
New York Central railroad....	1,602,197	331,075,547	$9,671,920	2.92 cents.
Erie railroad......................	3,242,792	478,485,772	11,611,023	2.45 "
Canals........	5,775,220	1,012,448,034	10,160,051	1.00 "
Totals.........	10,620,209	1,822,209,353	$31,442,994	1.18 "

The above table "shows that the cost of transportation on the canals, including the carrier's charges, is not one-half of the cost of railroad transits. This to some extent can be attributed to the fact that a larger proportion of low priced and low rated freights is carried on the canals than on the railroads.

But if the classes of freights, prices and rates were equal in their proportions between the canal and rail, the rail transportation would be one hundred per cent. above the canal. This the producer loses, or the consumer pays, on all rail transits, when that mode of carriage is preferred to canals."

It shows also that the canal during seven and a half months of the year, transported nearly a million tons more than two double track railroads between the same points did in twelve months, and did it at less than half the cost.

It is simply fatuity then to deride and undervalue canals because they are slower than railroads. It would take at least five railroads to do the heavy freighting business that could be done at half price by the canal; and if the canal were constructed, it would by its development of the mining and manufacturing interest of the country west of Buchanan, create business enough for two or three railroads.

The canal would carry the heavy freight that could not be profitably transported on the railroads, and the railroads would monopolize the merchandize and other freight demanding rapid transportation, which the canal could never take from them. All would get their own, and still there would be a demand for more channels of communication for the illimitable and ever increasing products of the west.

Mr. McAlpine in his report of 1853, conceded that "the dividing line of trade between the Virginia and the New York canals, when the former, and the enlargement of the Erie canal are completed, will be 110 miles north of Portsmouth and Cincinnati." That was before the contemplated enlargement of the Virginia canal. If his calculations had been based on a canal through Virginia of greater capacity than the Erie canal, he no doubt would have conceded all that is now claimed for it.

In the annual statement of the trade and commerce of Buffalo for the year 1865, reported for the Buffalo Board of Trade, by Mr. E. H. Walker, there is an interesting review of the commerce of the lakes and Erie canal and the competing routes, and first amongst the competing water routes, he places the James River and Kanawha canal, of which he says:

"Were this canal as large as the present Erie canal, notwithstanding its numerous locks, and its nearly 1900 feet of lockage lift, about the same as that of the Gennesse Valley Canal, it would, from its being open nearly all the year, be a strong competitor for the trade of the western states. The Ohio river is as free as the lakes, with the distance from the Mississippi to Point Pleasant, about the same as from the Mississippi to Buffalo. The states west of the Mississippi, including Missouri and Iowa, and those states immediately west of these states on the Missouri, as well as the southern portions of Illinois, Indiana and Ohio, and Kentucky, would be more immediately tributary to the James River and Kanawha Canal, than to the Erie, unless ship canals should be constructed through Ohio and Indiana."

The Hon. Israel D. Andrews, in his valuable report on Colonial and Lake trade, says of the James River and Kanawha Canal:

"Could this canal be carried into the Ohio valley with a sufficient supply of water, there can be no doubt it would become a route of an immense commerce. It would strike the Ohio at a very favorable point for *through* business. It would have this great advantage over the more northern works of a similar kind, that it would be navigable during the winter as well as the summer.

The route after crossing the Alleghany mountains is vastly rich in coal and iron, as well as in a very productive soil. Nothing seems to be wanting to the triumphant success of the work but a continuous water line to the Ohio."

It is a significant fact as to the appreciation of canals at the north, that although the state of New York has expended $55,000,000 in the construction of canals, and $32,000,000 in the enlargement of the Erie Canal, it is now recommended to spend $12,000,000 more in the further enlargement of the locks on that canal so as to pass boats of 500 tons burden, with a view of counteracting the effects of the projected ship canal around Niagara Falls, which would divert the trade of the lakes from the Erie canal to the St. Lawrence river.

It is also proposed to construct a ship canal from Chicago through the state of Illinois, by enlarging the present canal 100 miles in length, and improving the Illinois river, in order to connect lake Michigan with the lower Mississippi.

The proposed improvement is one of great magnitude, the locks of which are to be 350 feet long by 70 feet wide, and will involve an expenditure of $10,000,000.

A survey has been made for a ship canal from lake Michigan to lake Erie, and a charter granted by the Legislature of New York to a ship canal company for the construction of this work, with a capital stock of $25,000,000.

Canada is projecting a new canal from lake Huron by way of Ottawa river to Montreal, which is estimated to cost $24,000,000. The saving in distance between Montreal and Chicago by this direct route, almost due east from the straits of Mackinac, is 842 miles over that by the present circuitous line through the lower lakes and the St. Lawrence. The locks on this canal are to be 250 feet long by 50 feet wide, and ten feet on the sills, passing vessels of 1000 tons burden.

Another proposed ship canal is from Georgian bay, an outlet of lake Huron, by way of lake Simcoe to Toronto on lake Ontario, a distance of 100 miles. The proposed size of the locks is 265 feet in length by 55 feet in width, and the estimated cost of the improvement is $22,000,000.

The distance from Chicago to Liverpool by this route, as compared with that via Buffalo, is 837 miles less, and 428 miles less than the route by the Welland canal to Quebec.

These proposed canals and those already constructed and in operation, have all one purpose in view, "to attract to Canadian channels the products of the western states destined for the eastern seaboard." [E. H. Walker's report.]

It will thus be seen that New York and Canada are proposing to spend about $100,000,000 in enlarging present canals and constructing new ones, and all for the single purpose of drawing to their ports the great trade of the western states.

Virginia, which has the route that is shortest, best and longest open, should lose no time and spare no effort to secure this valuable prize.

SAVING TO THE WEST BY THE COMPLETION OF THE VIRGINIA CANAL.

But it is not Virginia alone that is interested in the completion of her water-line. To the western and northwestern states it is a matter of paramount importance. These states demand both a speedy and a cheap transit for their exports and imports. They have now the railroads with their quick transits but enormous charges, and the river route with its lower charges, but long time and other disadvantages that have been pointed out and are well understood. The Virginia water-line offers them the double inducement of rates lower than either the railroad or river routes, and an advantage in time and security from damage over the latter, which will insure to it the preference for the transportation of grain and provisions.

San Francisco, St. Louis and Richmond are nearly on the same parallel of latitude, and a line drawn through these cities is nearly the central line of the United States, and will be the central line of the trade of the world. All that is needed is the completion of eighty miles of canal, and the improvement of the natural water courses, to have a navigable water-line from Liverpool to Omaha, nearly due west, 5900 miles long.

This striking feature in this route, together with its having the most accessible, capacious, safe and deep harbor on the Atlantic coast, cannot fail to make it, if once completed, the great highway of traffic and emigration from Europe to the western states.

At a moderate calculation the amount that would be saved to the west by this route would be an average of $2 per ton on the river route, and at least $10 per ton over the railroad lines.

It' is no exaggeration to say that $40,000,000 a year could be saved to the west by the completion of the Virginia water-line on the freight that would pass over that route, besides a yield of 10 or 15 per cent. interest on the capital invested in the improvement. But the effect of the completion of the Virginia water-line will be not only to open a cheaper route for transportation from the west, but to reduce the charges on all the competing lines, and thereby lessen the cost of transportation on the whole trade of the west, to the extent probably of *one hundred million dollars per annum.*

I have thus endeavored in as brief a manner as possible, to give the history and character of the Virginia water-line, with my own views in regard to the manner in which it should be completed, and the advantages that it will then possess over other lines of communication with the west.

This latter part of the subject I have barely touched upon. To elucidate it fully would require more time than I could well spare from my other duties. I therefore leave it to you or to others to present the political, economical and commercial aspects of this question to the consideration of the people of the west, with the hope that a full understanding of its merits will lead to a speedy completion of this great work.

Very respectfully,

E. LORRAINE,
Chief Engineer J. R. & K. Co.